THE WHITE ELEPHANT CAPER
Georgette Livingston

Calico is holding a six-day spectacular over Labor Day, but there's more than just festivities going on in this sleepy little Nebraska town. First of all, there's the sudden appearance of counterfeit money, and the equally sudden appearance of Paul Bishop, a handsome blond-haired man with a beautiful dog named Casey. Next, there's the picture that veterinarian Jennifer Gray bought from Elmer Dodd that he is trying to buy back at a much higher price.

Attracted to a possible counterfeiter, and the owner of a painting in great demand, Jennifer doesn't exactly know what is going on . . . but she is determined to find out!

Cover illustration by Ernest Albanese
Cover design by Gordon Haber

THE WHITE ELEPHANT CAPER

•

(Book Nine)
in
**The Jennifer Gray
Veterinarian Mystery
Series**

•

GEORGETTE LIVINGSTON

AVALON BOOKS
THOMAS BOUREGY AND COMPANY, INC.
401 LAFAYETTE STREET
NEW YORK, NEW YORK 10003

PRINTED IN THE UNITED STATES OF AMERICA
ON ACID-FREE PAPER
BY HADDON CRAFTSMEN, BLOOMSBURG, PENNSYLVANIA

For Pat Armstrong, who is always an inspiration

Chapter One

"Wait until you see your next patient," Tina Allen said with a sly smile. "He's in the first examining room with his owner."

Jennifer Gray looked up from the mound of paperwork on her desk, and frowned. "We don't have any appointments scheduled for the rest of the morning, Tina, and we close in an hour, so unless it's an emergency . . ."

Tina tossed her head of brown, curly hair, and her eyes danced. "It isn't an emergency, Jennifer, but I just couldn't turn him away."

"Where is Ben?"

"In his office, buried under stacks of paperwork."

Jennifer waved an arm at the clutter on her desk. "And what does this look like to you?"

Tina scooted out, tossing over her shoulder, "I'll tell Mr. Bishop you'll be with him in a sec."

Perplexed, Jennifer stood up and stretched. They had been working long, difficult hours at the clinic for the last week, so that they could close up early for the holiday weekend, and she couldn't imagine what had gotten into the girl. Jennifer had no doubt in her mind that Tina was going to make a fine vet. She was bright, intelligent, and was wonderful when it came to following instructions, so what on earth had possessed her to admit an animal without an appointment, when it wasn't an emergency?

Changing into a clean blue lab coat, Jennifer reluctantly headed for the examining room. She didn't know anyone named Bishop, but then the town was overflowing with tourists, so Mr. Bishop was obviously one of them.

Trying for a courteous, professional smile, Jennifer walked into the examining room, not knowing what to expect, and was therefore totally unprepared for the sight before her. The dog was a gorgeous golden retriever, and the man matched the dog. Tall, lean, tan, and with a head of golden, wavy hair. But Mr. Bishop's eyes were sapphire blue instead of brown. He was wearing dark blue slacks, a blue polo shirt the color of his eyes, and she could smell the musky scent of his cologne.

"Mr. Bishop," Jennifer said, wondering why her voice sounded as though it had just gone through a blender at high speed. "What seems to be the problem?"

Tina, who was grinning from ear to ear, spoke up. "The dog's name is Casey, and I've already taken his temperature. It's normal." She looked up at Mr. Bishop adoringly, and bounced out.

Jennifer cleared her throat. "Well, if his temperature is normal, it can't be too serious."

The man gave her a lopsided grin, exposing one elongated dimple. "I didn't figure it was, but Casey means everything to me, and I didn't want to take any chances. He hasn't had much of an appetite, for one thing, Miss . . ." His eyes flickered over the nameplate attached to her lapel. ". . . Miss Gray. Or is it Dr. Gray? The vet I use at home is a good friend, so I call him by his name, which happens to be Hank. Or maybe you'd rather be called 'Ms.' Can't be 'Mrs.,' because I don't see a ring."

Jennifer noted the quick rush of color to his cheeks, and couldn't hold back the smile. "Whatever makes you comfortable, Mr. Bishop. If you'll put Casey on the table, I'll get on with the examination."

The man scooped up Casey in his arms with ease, placed him on the table, and when the dog stretched out on his side, he chuckled. ''Casey never has minded being inside a vet's office. I think it must be in his genes. His mother belonged to a vet.''

''What are you feeding him?'' Jennifer asked, looking into Casey's eyes with a small flashlight, and then down his throat.

''Kibbles 'n' Bits. Oh, and Kal Kan, too. I just sort of mix it all up together, and I never forget his vitamins. A couple of times a week I add in cottage cheese and some vegetables, and now and again a raw egg, though I've been told that's not a good idea. Something about the raw egg whites sapping out necessary vitamins.''

''Sounds like a good diet to me,'' Jennifer said, ''and I wouldn't worry too much about giving him an occasional raw egg. For years, raw eggs have been erroneously considered harmful to dogs because the egg white contains an enzyme, avidin, which will destroy a B-complex vitamin, biotin. But the truth is a dog would have to consume at least six or more eggs a day for a prolonged period of time for it to have harmful effects. Any vomiting?''

''No, but his breath is bad, and he's been restless at night. We're staying at the hotel, so I guess it's possible he feels a bit confined, but he's always been a good traveler before.''

''I see he's neutered. How old is he?''

''Almost five.''

Casey was watching Jennifer with trusting brown eyes, and his long, feathered tail wagged merrily as she looked at his teeth. ''He has some tartar on his teeth, which could account for the bad breath, and if he's showing signs of restlessness, I can certainly understand that. A dog like Casey needs a lot of room to run.''

''I live in upstate New York, and Casey has plenty of room to run when we're home,'' he replied easily.

''Well, if you're traveling by car, I can only hope it isn't a tiny compact.''

He smiled. ''I'm driving a van, and we make frequent stops, though I'll admit this particular venture has taken a lot longer than I expected.''

Jennifer took several instruments out of a drawer, and began to scrape the tartar off Casey's teeth. ''You're a long way from home, Mr. Bishop. Are you on vacation?''

''Call me Paul, please, and I guess you could call it a vacation, with a little business thrown in. I was on my way to Hot Springs, South Dakota, to look at some property when I found out about the fair here, and thought it sounded like fun. And from what I've seen, a lot of other people must've thought so, too. I've heard some of Calico's residents are even renting out rooms because the hotel and motel are full.''

''Yes, they are, and we've opened up a campground on a plot of land near the motel to accommodate the visitors with RVs. We expected a good turnout, but nothing like this, though I guess it shouldn't be a surprise when you consider our illustrious newspaper has been busy spreading the word for the last two weeks by sending out press releases and flyers.''

''Uh-huh, and that's how I found out about it. I was in North Platte and saw a flyer tacked to a telephone pole. It was bright yellow with black printing, and catchy. Said Calico—situated in the beautiful, inspiring, northwest corner of Nebraska—was holding a six-day 'spectacular' over Labor Day, which included a fair, dog show, white elephant sale, a dance, and a barbecue. It also said the town had recently experienced a major flood, and desperately needed the support of its fellow 'cornhuskers.' Though I don't know if I can believe that part of it. From what I've seen, the town looks in good shape to me.''

''That's because you haven't looked in the right places, and you don't know what the town looked like before the flood, Mr. Bishop . . . Paul. Fortunately, most of the major flooding was confined to an area northwest of town, but almost everybody was affected in one way or another. Many crops were ruined as a result, and we've had a considerable amount of water damage, but with a lot of prayers and hard work, we survived.''

"Well, thank goodness for that. It's a beautiful town. Were you born here?''

Jennifer nodded. ''I was orphaned at a very young age, and my grandfather and his housekeeper, Emma Morrison, raised me. Grandfather is pastor of the Calico Christian Church. If you're around on Monday, you'll probably meet him. He's in charge of the barbecue. Emma, like the rest of us, is helping out where she can. It's a very busy time, but well worth the effort.''

He looked around at the spacious well-equipped room. ''And do you own the Front Street veterinary clinic?''

"No, my associate Ben Copeland owns it, though I'll be taking over when he retires in a few years.''

He nodded at a framed photo on the wall. ''It's just a guess, but I'd say the rugged-looking man is Ben Copeland. He looks like my idea of a country vet. Able to wrestle a cow to the ground, and sit on a bull if he has to.''

He was referring to the photo on the wall taken of Ben and several town dignitaries at the ribbon-cutting ceremonies for the clinic's grand opening. "That's Ben. The photo was taken about twenty years ago, but he hasn't changed, though his hair might be a little grayer. He's a wonderful man, and yes, he could sit on a bull if he had to."

"And the young lady with the captivating smile who was in here earlier?"

"That's Tina Allen. We hired her last year to help out around the clinic, and she's become our third set of hands. She wants to be a veterinarian, so we'll be losing her next year to college, and then vet school. And believe me, she'll be sorely missed.

"Come on, Casey, open wider."

"He likes you," Paul said. "But then he's always been partial to pretty women."

Warmed by the compliment, Jennifer stroked the dog's head. "Well, I like him, too. He's a lovely animal. Is he up on his shots?"

"Yes, ma'am."

Jennifer gritted her teeth. *Ma'am?* It made her feel ancient. "Call me Miss, Ms., Doctor, or Jennifer, but *please* don't call me ma'am!"

He grinned, and gave her a little salute. "Then it'll be 'Jennifer.' "

He said her name with so much affection, she felt the tips of her ears burn. "Ah, well, I see he's wearing tags. Have you ever considered using a microchip for identification? It would be a big help in the event Casey ever gets lost and loses his collar. Or if he's stolen. I know that's a gruesome thought, but it happens, especially when an animal is a purebred, and worth bucks. The culprits remove the collar and tags, leaving no way to identify the animal. Tattoos can be used effectively, too, but a tattoo is usually put on the inside of the ear, and there have been cases where the culprits have lopped off an ear to get rid of the evidence.''

Paul shuddered. ''Sounds more than gruesome, but then, so does the use of a microchip. I know we live in a world filled with space-age technology, but I'm not so sure I'd like to have Casey turned into a bionic dog.''

Jennifer smiled. ''The microchip is about the size of a grain of rice, and it's inserted under the animal's skin with a needle. It's a painless procedure, has no side effects, is quite inexpensive, and the chip will remain in the dog until he dies. The purpose is simple. All the pertinent information about the animal, including its owner, is on the chip, and it can be scanned, or read, by veterinarians, animal pounds, shelters, and so on. It's a very good way of recording permanent identification, and can be used on any animal when deemed necessary.''

''Amazing.''

"Yes, it certainly is." She stood back. "That should about do it." She reached in another drawer and handed Paul a cellophane-wrapped toothbrush. "Giving Casey a dog biscuit or two a day is one way to help keep the tartar from building up, and brushing his teeth is another."

Paul looked at the toothbrush, and shook his head. "Oh, brother. Now I've heard of everything."

"Uh-huh, and someday, when Casey is an old dog and still has all his teeth, he'll thank you. Tartar buildup can cause all sorts of problems, like abscesses and gum disease. Some people use regular toothpaste, but as a rule dogs hate the taste, so mixing up a simple solution of a teaspoon of salt and a teaspoon of baking soda in a cup of water will work just as well. The gums might bleed for the first few brushings, but that's to be expected, and it won't hurt him."

Paul stuck the toothbrush in a back pocket, and said, "So, can you put it in?"

"The microchip? I'd be happy to, but I simply don't have the time. We all have a bezillion things to do between now and tomorrow morning when the fair officially opens, and that's why we're closing the clinic at noon today, and won't open again until Tuesday morning, unless, of course, we have an emergency. If you're serious about wanting the implant, I would suggest you talk to your vet friend Hank when you get home, and go from there.''

Paul looked disappointed. ''So, with you being so busy and all, I don't suppose you'd have the time to join me for lunch? Or maybe a cup of coffee? I've already staked out Kelly's Coffee Shop, and the food is great. Can't say much for the coffee, but I learned a long time ago, we can't have everything.''

Truly tempted, Jennifer thought about it for a moment, and finally shook her head. ''I'd better not. I'm working at the white elephant sale this afternoon, and I can eat there. It's being held in Calico Park on the terrace in front of the senior citizens' center, and they've cooked up enough food to feed most of Nebraska.'' She ruffled Casey's fur, watched the disappointment on Paul's face grow, and took a deep breath. ''Of course, you could always join me, and maybe even have lunch there. They are only charging a dollar a plate, and it's really quite good.''

Paul's smile was as bright as the early September sun. ''You've got a deal, unless dogs aren't allowed.''

''And what would you do with Casey if you had lunch at Kelly's?''

''Park right out front, leave him in the van with the windows down, sit where I could watch him, and take him a hamburger.''

Jennifer looked down at the dog fondly. "And you're spoiled, too. Well, you can just tell your master that with the exception of our restaurants, the market, and the ice cream parlor, well-behaved dogs are welcome almost everywhere in Calico, as long as they are on a leash."

"Then it's a date," Paul said exuberantly. "What time?"

"I have to finish up some paperwork first, so let's make it around one. My shift doesn't start until two, so that will give us an hour."

His face fell. "Only an hour, huh? That's hardly enough time to eat, let alone get acquainted."

Not knowing how to respond to that, short of inviting him to spend the afternoon with her while she worked, Jennifer finally quipped, "Well, I guess we'll just have to eat fast. I'll meet you on the terrace at one. Do you need directions?"

Paul shook his head. "I was there yesterday, while they were setting up."

After Paul Bishop paid his bill and left the clinic, Jennifer went back to her office wondering if she was losing her mind. The man was a stranger. She knew absolutely nothing about him, and yet the thought of spending some time with him, even an hour, made her a little light-headed. It also left her wondering how she could have missed him yesterday, because she, too, had been at the park for an hour or so while they were setting up.

Jennifer was in her office, trying to concentrate on the paperwork, when Tina bounded in, barely able to contain her excitement. "So, what did you think of him? Isn't he gorgeous?"

Ben followed Tina into the office, and his smile was warm and wide. "I don't think she's talking about the dog, Jennifer. I think she's referring to the owner. She says she's in love."

Jennifer couldn't help but smile. "Casey is a beautiful animal, and Mr. Bishop is a very nice man."

"And?" Tina said a little breathlessly.

Jennifer shrugged. "I scraped tartar off Casey's teeth, gave Paul some instructions, and . . ."

"Ah-ha!" Tina exclaimed. "Did you hear that, Ben? She called him 'Paul'! So, where is he from and what does he do? Is he in town for the fair? How long is he going to stay, and—"

Jennifer raised a hand. "Whoa, Tina, slow down! We weren't in the examining room more than fifteen minutes. Hardly enough time for the Inquisition. He's from upstate New York, he was on his way to South Dakota to look at some property when he found out about the fair, and thought it sounded like fun. That's it.''

Tina's mouth drew down in a pout. "Well, if I'd been in your shoes, I would've found out *everything* about him.''

"So, what was wrong with the dog?" Ben asked. "Other than having tartar on his teeth.''

"He hasn't been eating well, and he seems restless. It would be my guess, Casey is simply getting bored with the trip and the confines of the van, and wants to go home.''

"Then Mr. Bishop drove all the way from New York?" Ben asked.

"Yes, and he also said the trip has taken a lot longer than he expected. I have the feeling after he looks at the property in South Dakota, he'll head home.''

Ben said, "What part of South Dakota?''

"Hot Springs.'' Jennifer looked at her watch, and stuffed the papers on her desk in a folder. "I guess there isn't anything here that can't wait until Tuesday. I'm meeting Paul for lunch at one, and want to go home first and freshen up.''

Tina gave a little gasp. "You're having lunch with him!''

Ben teased, "Looks like he made a lasting impression on somebody else. Better close your mouth, Tina, before you swallow a fly.''

Jennifer frowned. "You two are simply too

much. Well, thank goodness Grandfather and Emma are out and about, so I don't have to go through this again when I go home to change my clothes.''

Tina's eyes twinkled. ''You hear that, Ben? She's even going to change her clothes.''

''I heard.'' Ben took off his lab coat, and draped it over an arm. ''If I don't see you ladies before tomorrow, I'll see you at the fair. Irene talked me into going into the 'dunk tank', and like always, I gave her an automatic yes without thinking. That's what happens when you've been married for thirty-five years.''

Tina smiled slyly. ''I'm working at the petting zoo most of the morning, so be sure and stop by, Jennifer. Then you can tell me all about your date with Paul Bishop.''

Jennifer shook her head. ''It isn't a date, Tina. I'm simply having lunch with the man.''

Tina gave her a cunning look. ''Methinks thou dost protest too much, Miss Gray, and no matter what you say, I call it a date. See you guys tomorrow.''

Ben waited until Tina had gone before he said, ''What about Ken Hering, Jennifer? Or what about Willy? I think it was pretty admirable of Willy to stand aside when Ken came into your life, but do you think Ken will be as understanding?''

Jennifer rolled her eyes. "Not you, too!"

"Well, you have been dating Ken at a pretty steady clip, and although you say it isn't serious, I think it could be. Could have been serious with Willy, too, if you'd given it half a chance."

Exasperated, Jennifer scowled. "I don't want 'serious', Ben. I want carefree, uncomplicated relationships, based on friendship. I grew up with Willy Ashton, and I love him. But I'm not *in* love with him. He feels the same way about me, so why would he care who I date or why? And Ken is just a good friend. We have fun together, that's all, so why would he care if I have lunch with a man who happens to be visiting town on his way to South Dakota?"

"Well, best you remind yourself of that when you look in the mirror, and see what I'm looking at now. Your face is alive with anticipation, Jennifer, but you'd better remember Paul Bishop is just passing through. Here today, gone tomorrow."

Annoyed, Jennifer returned, "That's right. Here today and gone tomorrow, so what's the dig deal?"

"It won't be a big deal unless you turn it into one," Ben replied, giving her a hug. "And I'm sorry if I sound like an old mother hen. I guess all I'm trying to say is, it would break my heart to see you get hurt."

"And I love you for caring," Jennifer said, returning his hug, "even if you're worrying needlessly."

But later at home, after going through every outfit in her closet, trying to find something appropriate to wear, Jennifer finally caught her reflection in the mirror, and wondered if Ben's concerns might be justified after all. Her eyes were too bright, her cheeks much too flushed, and even her heartbeat was erratic.

Truly glad her grandfather and Emma were out and she was alone, Jennifer settled on a soft peach-colored sundress, brushed her golden hair a hundred strokes, and left the house with Ben's words of warning ringing in her ears.

The senior citizens' center, officially called Calico House, was a low, sprawling structure with large windows. A flagstone terrace not only stretched across the front, but reached all the way to the rose gardens and the expanse of lush green lawn beyond where, at the moment, a good many visitors were stretched out on blankets, resting their feet and soaking up the sun. The terrace had been the ideal place to set up the white elephant sale, just as the patio area between Calico House and the creek was the perfect location to serve the food, giving the weary shoppers—residents and tourists alike—

a shady spot to eat and rest. Picnic tables, chairs, and colorful umbrellas had been set up everywhere, and for those who preferred a little more shade or solitude, wooden benches had been erected along the creek.

Unfortunately, parking all over town was a nightmare, so Jennifer decided to leave her Jeep Cherokee at home, and walk the four blocks to the park.

A little breathless from her quick pace, Jennifer waved at the people she knew, and looked for a head of golden-blond, wavy hair, towering above the crowd. *He's not that tall,* she reminded herself. Maybe six-two or three . . . She shook her head, and tried to focus her attention on the many tables heaped with odds and ends. Nearly everyone in Calico had donated something for the sale, but only a small handful had volunteered their time to work the tables, collect the money, and remind the people who considered it all junk, ''One person's junk can be another person's treasure.''

At the moment, Ben's wife, Irene, was arguing with an elderly couple over the price of a copper teapot, and when they moved on, Irene sighed. ''I've spent the whole morning trying to inform the dense multitude that our prices are fair, and all I've gotten in return are a lot of moans and groans. Do you think one dollar and fifty cents is too much for that teapot?''

Irene Copeland was a pretty, dark-haired woman who normally took problems, no matter how difficult, in her stride. But now, her face was lined with tension. ''Not at all,'' Jennifer replied, ''though I think twenty-five dollars might be a bit much for that painting propped up at the end of your table.''

Irene frowned. ''Well, I thought so, too, but Elmer Dodd wouldn't let me lower the price. He said that painting has been in his family for years, and is worth ten times that amount. I tried to remind him that this is supposed to be a fundraiser, but my words fell on deaf ears.''

Jennifer studied the not-so-good painting of an eagle soaring through the sky against a backdrop of high mountain country, and said, ''Well, at least he coughed up something. The last I heard, he wasn't going to donate anything because he thought the white elephant sale was a stupid idea. Though I suppose if he'd thought of it instead of Willy, it would've been a different story.''

''Uh-huh, well, Elmer coughed up more than the painting, Jennifer. Mary Ellis is manning a table down at the end of the line, and it's full of archaic things Elmer has had stored in his basement since his father passed away. Relics of the past, and most of it is ghastly, and over-priced. He wanted to spread it around. You know, put a few things on all the tables, but I refused. With the exception of the painting, I didn't want to deal with it, and it's a good thing. Mary says the people take one look at the stuff on her table, and walk away, shaking their heads.''

Jennifer reached into her purse, pulled out her billfold, and plunked twenty-five dollars on the table. ''Well, because fifty percent of each sale goes to the town, I'll take the painting. Maybe that will show up some of the holdouts, and rouse them into action. I know money is tight right now, but the whole idea of the white ele-phant sale was to put money in the town coffer. Leave the price tag on it, mark it sold, and keep it on display. You can even put my name on it, if you want.''

''Maybe you should look around first,'' Irene suggested. ''You could get a lot more for your money, and not everything is 'junk.' ''

Jennifer studied the painting. ''I realize it isn't a very good painting, but the eagle is nice, and the frame is attractive, so consider it sold.''

Irene shrugged. ''Suit yourself.''

''Jennifer . . .''

Jennifer recognized the voice, felt her heart flutter, and turned around. Apparently Paul had decided to freshen up, too, and was now wearing white. White ducks, a white polo shirt that brought out the dark sheen of his tan, and brown leather boat shoes. His gaze was roaming over her appreciatively, too, and her voice sounded shaky again when she said, "Hi! Have you been here long?"

"Not long. I was just looking at all the great stuff over there on the last table. Looks like most of it came out of a museum."

Jennifer leaned over and gave Casey a hug. In return, she received a happy slurp on the cheek. "You're talking about the dregs from Elmer Dodd's basement. He owns the dairy, and lives in a mansion across the river that is filled with antiques, bric-a-brac, and relics of the past. I've never been in the house, but I've heard he even has a suit of armor standing in the entry-way."

Irene cleared her throat, and Jennifer flushed. "Uh, this is Irene Copeland, Paul. She's Ben's wife. Irene, this is Paul Bishop. . . ."

Irene gave Paul a brilliant smile. "You know my husband?"

Paul returned her smile. "I haven't met him, but I was at the clinic earlier, and saw his picture hanging on the wall."

Irene peered over the table at Casey, and was met by a wagging tail. "Well, I certainly hope there is nothing wrong with your beautiful dog.''

"As it turns out, he's fine. Just a little weary from all the traveling, I would suspect. We're a long way from home." He nodded at the painting. "That's interesting."

The corners of Jennifer's mouth dimpled up in a grin. "Well, that's one way to put it. I just bought it, and don't you dare ask me why. It's from Elmer Dodd's collection of antiquities, too."

"That name is familiar," Paul said.

"He's running for mayor, and you've probably seen the banners and posters all over town."

He snapped his fingers. "That's it. The man with the beady eyes. I met his opponent this morning, and *he* would be my choice. Willy Ashton, attorney-at-law. The young man with an honest face and a solid handshake."

"Willy is a good friend," Jennifer said warmly, "and he'll make an outstanding mayor. Where did you meet him?"

"At the doughnut shop. I was talking to the clerk about the fair when Willy walked in. We were introduced, and the conversation went from there."

Irene said, "Well, Willy Ashton is a fine young man. It was his idea to hold the white elephant sale, though I'm beginning to wonder if it was such a good idea. Most of the folks aren't in a buying mood, and those who are, think the prices are too high.''

''Maybe you should consider bargaining,'' Paul said. ''Without fixed prices, it would be open for debate, and it seems to me no matter what they end up paying, it would be better than nothing, and for sure, it would be better than ending up with a lot of leftovers. I had a moving sale once. Half of everything I owned was all over the front lawn, and I'll never forget how I felt when the last car drove away, and half the stuff was still all over my lawn. I ended up calling a junk dealer to cart it off.''

At that moment, a young couple strolled up, and Paul whispered, ''Watch this.'' He picked up the teapot, and said, ''I can't believe you're letting this go for a buck and a half. Why, it's worth at least ten. This is a fund-raiser for the town, after all, and when you consider what hardships the residents have had to endure because of that harrowing flood, you'd think people would open their hearts as well as their wallets.'' He turned and looked at the young woman. ''What do you think, miss? Don't you think this teapot is worth at least ten dollars? There isn't a scratch on it, and the handle is in perfect shape.''

45664

"You've been wanting a copper teapot, Margie," the young man said, "and he's right. It's worth at least ten."

Margie smiled, reached in her purse, and pulled out a ten. "We'll take it."

After they'd paid for the teapot and walked off, Jennifer said, "That wasn't bargaining, Paul. That was just good salesmanship."

Irene nodded appreciatively. "It certainly was! How would you like to work one of the tables?"

"I have a better idea," Jennifer said, smiling up at him. "Would you consider working at my table this afternoon? I could sure use your help."

Paul's response was immediate. "Sorry, but something has come up, and I can't stay. We'll have to take a rain check on lunch, too, Jennifer. Sorry."

More than surprised, Jennifer tried to hide her disappointment, and muttered, "So am I."

Paul fished in a pocket, pulled out a twenty-dollar bill, and handed it to Irene. "The young couple gave you a ten, so if you have another ten in your receipt box, would you mind if I give you this twenty in exchange?"

"No problem," Irene said, handing him the two tens. But after he gave them a quick nod and hurried off, she frowned. "That sure was strange."

"I was just thinking the same thing," Jennifer replied, watching the tall blond man and his dog disappear into the crowd.

"I take it you were planning to have lunch together?"

"Yes, we were. He wanted to go to Kelly's, but I didn't have the time because I was expected to start my shift at two. I told him there was plenty of food here, and we agreed to meet at one, which would have given us an hour. . . ." She closed her eyes, trying to remember his words. "When he found out we were only going to have an hour, he said, 'Only an hour, huh? That's hardly enough time to eat, let alone get acquainted.' Oh, and earlier, when I suggested he might consider having a microchip implanted in his dog for permanent identification, he asked me if I could do it. I told him I couldn't because we were closing the clinic at noon for the holiday. At that point in time, he certainly didn't appear to be a man in a hurry. And wouldn't you think if he'd had a change of plans, he would have said something to me the minute he got here, instead of casually talking about Elmer Dodd's relics, the mayoral race, and the teapot?"

Irene pursed her lips. "Maybe we said something that upset him?"

Jennifer didn't know what to think, nor could she explain how she felt. She was disappointed, but it was more than that. It was like everything was slightly off kilter, like she'd missed something important, leaving her with a deep sense of foreboding that was as dark as a midwinter day.

Chapter Two

It was almost six o'clock when Jennifer wearily walked into the comfortable house she shared with her grandfather and Emma. But it wasn't until she joined them in the cozy yellow kitchen, and saw their wonderful, loving faces, that the tears she had been holding back for hours finally slipped down her cheeks.

"Lordy, what on earth!" Emma exclaimed, wiping her hands on her apron.

Alarmed, Wesley Gray jumped up from the table. "Good heavens, sweetheart. What is it?"

Thoroughly embarrassed, and confused by her irrational behavior, Jennifer dropped to a chair, and muttered, "It's been a horrible day. Sorry.

27

I didn't mean to come in blubbering like a fool and upset everything.''

Emma handed Jennifer a box of tissues, and scowled. ''You don't take to tears easily, young lady, so whatever happened must have been pretty bad. Well, you just sit there and relax while I fix you a cup of tea.''

Wes sat down across from Jennifer, and took her hand. ''Maybe you've been trying to do too much, sweetheart. I was telling Emma just a few minutes ago that I think we'd all better sit back and catch our breaths. I've been on the go since seven this morning, and feel like I'm a hundred and ten. And I'm not alone. Half the town is going around bone-weary, and are either in a daze or disgruntled. Not much point in putting money in the town's coffer if nobody is going to be alive to enjoy the profits.''

''It's even beginning to get to the Cromwell sisters,'' Emma said. ''They were at the Grange today, helping out, and they fought the whole time. I know squabbling is like second nature to them, but this was different. I also got the distinct feeling that Fanny wasn't feeling well, and poor little Peaches. She was so upset, she spent one solid hour screeching at the top of her lungs, and believe me, there is nothing worse than a screeching chimpanzee. Most of those out-of-town arts and crafts people had already pulled in, and I could tell they were wondering if they'd made a mistake, signing on for the fair. I heard one woman who sells jewelry tell a man who sells posters, that she hates working in small towns, because all the people are 'weirdos.' I felt like telling her nobody was twisting her arm to stay. Anyway, when I left, Frances was trying to talk Fanny into going home, and Peaches was hiding under a table, sulking.''

"It's getting to Willy, too," Wes said, "and you know Willy. He usually manages to stay calm through just about anything. He got into a shouting match with Collin Dodd this afternoon, and all I can say is, it's a good thing a bunch of us were there when it happened, or they probably would have ended up using fisticuffs. Collin said his uncle should be commended because he donated so many priceless antiques to the white elephant sale, when all Willy donated was an out-of-print book and a few rusty tools. Collin said his uncle was so generous because he cares about the town, and that's why he's going to get elected mayor. Willy kept his humor throughout the whole incident, and probably would've walked away, if Collin hadn't kept pushing, and finally accused Willy of flirting with all the women in town to get their votes. That's when I knew we were in for trouble, but before I could intervene, the shouting match was on. I won't go into the details, but suffice it to say, I don't think I've ever seen Willy angrier. I also think it might have been a setup, because along about that time Ken Hering showed up with his trusty camera, so I would imagine we'll be reading all about it in the morning paper. Anything to put Willy in a bad light.''

Emma placed a cup of tea in front of Jennifer, and clucked her tongue. "Ken might be a reporter for *The Calico Review*, and *The Calico Review* might be backing Elmer Dodd, but Ken hasn't tried to hide the fact he's in Willy's corner.''

"That might be true, Emma, but Ken is a good reporter, and he's got himself one whale of a story. If you were in his shoes, how would you handle it?''

Jennifer looked at her grandfather's handsome face, noted the fresh sunburn across his forehead, which looked quite angry against his head of wavy gray hair, and sighed. "Well, if you're trying to make me forget my dreadful day, you're succeeding. By the way, your forehead is sunburned, Grandfather. Better put something on it.''

Emma harrumphed and stabbed at a tomato. "That's what I've been telling him for the last hour. So what does he do? He turns it all around and tells me my sprained ankle is a lot more serious than a body getting too much sun.''

Jennifer exclaimed, ''Oh, Emma! You sprained your ankle?''

''Well, it isn't exactly a sprain. I just twisted it a bit while I was trying to help get some tables set up at the Grange. *My* mistake was telling him about it.''

''I told her she should stay off her feet,'' Wes said. ''But you know Emma. The kitchen and meal preparation is her domain, and heaven help the person who tries to change her mind.''

''That's right, and I told him phooey! I still have a million and one things to do before tomorrow morning, and I'm not an invalid. I'm not even limping.''

Wes returned, ''A twisted ankle isn't a laughing matter, Emma, and when you get out of bed tomorrow morning and fall flat on your face, you'll be sorry you didn't take my advice.''

Jennifer smiled for the first time in hours. ''Well, I guess this is as good a time as any to tell you we are now the proud owners of one of Elmer Dodd's 'priceless antiques.' I left it in the living room.''

When Jennifer started to get up, Wes raised a hand. ''You sit still, sweetheart. If you had the courage to bring it home, I've got the courage to go get it.''

Emma groaned. "Lordy, I can't imagine."

"Well, it isn't too bad, Emma, though it *was* overpriced."

A few minutes later, after Wes had returned with the painting and Emma got a good look at it, she rolled her eyes. "How much?"

"I paid twenty-five dollars for it, but I had a good reason."

Emma spouted, "Well, if you want my opinion, five dollars would've been too much. Some of the senior citizens who are taking the beginners art class at Calico House can do better than that!"

Wes held up the painting, and studied it for a moment before placing it on a chair. "Oh, I don't know, Emma. It isn't great, but it isn't all that bad either. The eagle looks like an eagle, and the frame looks like it's a genuine antique. You know, I think I saw this painting hanging above the fireplace in Elmer's father's bedroom. That was in the old house when he was ailing, and Elmer thought a few prayers might be in order."

Emma was working on a cucumber now, and turning it into mush. "If you're talking about that time just before Elmer's daddy died, that was a long time ago, Wes."

Wes grinned. "I've been trying to tell you even though my hearing might be a little off, and my eyesight isn't what it used to be, I still have a good memory. After his father died, this painting probably went down in the basement with all the other relics.''

''I never could figure out why Elmer took along all his father's things when he built that house across the river for Bernice,'' Emma said. ''Especially when Bernice hated every single bit of it, and was continually after him to get rid of what she considered 'the whole unsightly mess.' ''

''Maybe Elmer thought 'the whole unsightly mess' would be worth big bucks someday,'' Jennifer said thoughtfully. ''And we all know how he is when it comes to money.''

''Unscrupulous, just like his daddy,'' Emma said. But when she turned around, there was a frown on her face. ''So if that's the reason he's hung on to it all, all these years, why did he donate so much of it to the white elephant sale? Even if every bit of it sells, he'll still only be getting fifty percent.''

''Fifty percent is better than nothing,'' Wes reasoned, ''and then we have Collin to consider. He's been living with his uncle for almost a year now, and from what I've heard, he's talked Elmer into making a lot of changes in the Dodd mansion. I'm sure he's thinking ahead. Like if Elmer is elected mayor, they'll be moving into the mayor's house, and it's already furnished. I can see him talking Elmer into selling the mansion, too, and it would be a lot easier to do if it wasn't full of junk. Better to get rid of it this way, and claim he's doing it 'for the town.' Anything to get a few more votes. If you'll notice, I didn't say 'when' Elmer is elected mayor. I said 'if,' but it doesn't take much to figure out the Dodd kind of logic and reasoning.''

Emma looked down her nose at Jennifer. ''You said you had a good reason for buying that painting, young lady. Are you going to tell us what that reason is?''

After Jennifer explained, Wes said, ''So, did your plan work?''

Jennifer sighed. ''No, unfortunately, it backfired. The SOLD sign on the painting, along with my name, did nothing more than put me under the gun all afternoon. Not with the tourists, but every Calico resident who happened by either wanted to know if I'd lost my mind, or if I was now backing Elmer Dodd in the mayoral race.''

Emma dumped the tomatoes and cucumbers into a bowl, added a bit of tarragon vinegar and sugar, and said, ''So, is that the reason for all the tears?''

Jennifer lowered her eyes. ''I guess it was part of it.''

Wes said, ''And the rest?''

Jennifer finished the tea, and considered her response. She didn't want to upset them, but she didn't want to keep it from them, either. She needed their guidance, for one thing, and she supposed she needed their assurance that she wasn't going mad. She took a deep breath. "I met a man today. Actually, it was at the clinic, just before we closed at noon. I'm not going to put the blame on Tina, even though she was the one who let him in when she shouldn't have, because it wasn't an emergency. . . . Well, what can I say? She was taken with the man and his dog, but then, so was I."

Emma was working on the cooked chicken now, removing the skin and bones, but she was listening. And so was Wes, and his blue eyes were filled with concern.

Jennifer felt hot spots touch her cheeks. "I can see you're disturbed, Grandfather, and I understand. You're wondering how a man and his dog can walk into the clinic at a little before noon, and by six o'clock the same day, he's managed to turn me into a sniffling wreck. I might be able to answer that if we'd spent the afternoon together. But we didn't. I spent fifteen minutes with him at the clinic, and maybe twenty minutes with him at the park, and I haven't seen him since. That's it."

Emma said, "Park. What park?"

"Calico Park. He wanted to take me to lunch at Kelly's, but I couldn't go because I had to work at the white elephant sale. I told him about the senior citizens serving food, so we agreed to meet at the park at one, which would have given us an hour. I was with Irene when he got there, and twenty minutes later, he was gone. He said something came up, and we'd have to take a rain check on lunch. That's it."

Emma looked at Wes. "She keeps saying 'that's it,' but I get the distinct feeling that isn't 'it.' What else happened, Jennifer?"

"Nothing else happened, and that's why I feel like such a fool. It shouldn't have affected me this way, and I don't know why it did."

Wes said, "Okay, let's back up. What's the man's name, sweetheart?"

"Paul Bishop. He was in North Platte when he found out about our Labor Day festivities, and thought it sounded like fun. He's staying at the hotel."

"And?" Wes asked.

Jennifer shrugged. "If I say 'that's it' again, Emma is going to scream. But truly, that's it. His dog wasn't feeling well, he brought him into the clinic, and . . ."

Emma harrumphed. "And that's it. So, is this man, this Paul Bishop, from North Platte?"

"No, Emma. He's from upstate New York.

He was in North Platte on his way to South Dakota to look at some property when he saw the flyer about our 'six-day spectacular' tacked to a telephone pole. He said he was on vacation, mixing business with pleasure, and I had no reason to doubt him. Nor did I have any reason to believe he was going to turn me into an emotional wreck. But that's my fault, not his.''

Emma scowled at Jennifer. ''You expect us to believe a perfect stranger could turn you into an emotional wreck within forty-five minutes?''

''Jennifer doesn't need to be reprimanded, Emma,'' Wes said stoutly.

''I'm not reprimanding her!'' Emma exclaimed. ''I'm simply trying to understand!''

Jennifer hated this whole discussion. She hated every sharp word. And it was her fault for coming home and dumping the subject in their laps. Emma and Wes could see she was upset, so there was no way she was going to compound it by having a temper tantrum or going off in a huff. Years ago, after her parents had been killed in an auto accident, that was the way she'd handled everything, even going so far as to run away. But that was then and this was now. She'd learned a lot of things over the years, the most important of which had been the value of truth and honesty, and the realization that she had two people who loved her. And oh, how she loved them!

Jennifer took a deep breath. "He walked into the clinic this morning and knocked my socks off," she said finally.

Emma's face softened. "Lordy, how could I forget. It was a long time ago, but the same thing happened to me. His name was Billy Docket. He came to town one day, and within ten minutes after meeting him, I just knew I was in love."

Wes lifted a brow. "Billy Docket? Wasn't he that musician who came through town on his way to California?"

Emma smiled. "Yes, he was, and I thought he was wonderful. Here today, gone tomorrow. I fell in love on Tuesday, and he was gone on Wednesday. I thought my heart would break."

Wes reasoned, "You can't fall in love with somebody that fast, Emma. It had to be a crush."

Emma sighed. "Call it what you will, Wes, but I was smitten, and miserable, all in a matter of twenty-four hours, and I just knew my life was over. Of course, that was before I realized broken hearts are counterproductive." She looked at Jennifer, and smiled. "I think everybody has to have that one person in their life who 'knocks their socks off,' Jennifer."

"Judy Cook," Wes said. "I was a freshman in high school the year she made head cheerleader, and I loved her from afar. She was going with some college guy from Nebraska State, and wouldn't give me the time of day."

"Judy Cook!" Emma exclaimed incredulously. "Why, she was nothing but a blond—I think she would be called an 'airhead' today."

Wes grinned. "No doubt, but I still thought I was in love. I couldn't eat or sleep, and my grades suffered. It wasn't until my dad pulled me up by the bootstraps and told me I was throwing my life away, that I came to my senses. By then, Judy Cook had run off with the college boy, and the last I heard, they have ten kids, seven grandkids, and Judy weighs three hundred pounds. The point is, sweetheart, I got over it, and so did Emma."

Jennifer shook her head. "You guys are talking about love, real or imaginary, but love doesn't enter into this."

Wes said, "Of course it doesn't, because love doesn't happen overnight. It has to be nurtured and allowed to grow into all that it was meant to be. But attraction can be instant and, very often, just as intense and confusing."

"So, what does this Paul Bishop look like?" Emma asked.

Trying to downplay the impact Paul Bishop

had had on her, but not at all sure if she could, Jennifer said, "Actually, Paul and his dog look a lot alike."

Emma tittered. "So, does this Paul Bishop have a tail?"

Jennifer laughed. "Well, of course they don't actually look alike, Emma, but the dog is a beautiful golden retriever, and Paul's hair is the same color. He's also very tall, very tan, and has blue eyes."

Wes's brow furrowed in thought. "A tall man with golden-colored hair. I saw him at the doughnut shop this morning, talking to Willy."

Emma's cheeks puffed out. "The doughnut shop? What were you doing at the doughnut shop, Wesley Gray?"

"Don't worry, Emma, I wasn't cheating on my diet. I stopped by to pick up an order of doughnuts for the senior citizens who got up at dawn to do all that cooking. Paul Bishop is a handsome man, though I didn't see the dog."

"I'm sure Casey was in the van," Jennifer said. "Paul told me about meeting Willy in the doughnut shop."

Emma said, "Speaking of boyfriends, how do you suppose Willy and Ken Hering are going to react when they find out a tall, handsome stranger has 'knocked your socks off'?"

Jennifer sighed. "You sound like Ben, and

I'll tell you what I told him. Willy and I are good friends, and he doesn't care who I date, and if you were to ask him, I'm sure you'd find Ken feels the same way. So, how could they possibly get upset over me seeing a man who isn't going to be in town for more than a few days at the most?''

"It would upset them if they thought you were going to get hurt," Emma reasoned.

"So, do I have to tell them how I feel?"

"So, how *do* you feel?" Wes asked. "I mean down deep, where it counts."

"Disappointed because Paul had to cancel our lunch date, and angry at myself for acting like such a twit. But there is something else. . . ."

"Boy oh boy," Wes said. "Here it comes."

"Unfortunately, I can't go into the specifics, because it's just a feeling. You know, when everything seems slightly off kilter, but you don't know why? I guess it wasn't so much the fact he broke our lunch date, it was the way he went about it. One minute we were smiling and talking to Irene, and then out of the blue, he announced something had come up and he couldn't stay. And it was the way he looked. His smile was gone, and there was something in his eyes. His behavior puzzled Irene, too, and she thought maybe we'd said something to upset him.''

"Maybe he was upset because he had to break your lunch date," Emma said.

"No, it was more than that. I watched him hurry off through the crowd, and I was left with such a deep sense of foreboding, it frightened me. I kept waiting for him to come back all afternoon, and I even considered stopping at the hotel to see him on my way home, but thought better of it. I wouldn't have known what to say to him without sounding like dimwit."

The next few minutes were silent while Emma cubed the chicken for the salad, and Wes played with the packets of Sweet 'n Low on the table. Finally Wes said, "Do you think you'd feel better or worse if you saw him again?"

"I can't honestly answer that, Grandfather. But I've already made up my mind if I run into him between now and Monday, I'm going to do my very best to ignore him. And Lord only knows, I'll have enough to keep me busy."

Emma said, "We all have enough to keep us busy. More than enough. I finally had to write down our schedules so I'd have it clear in my mind, and I'm already exhausted."

Wes pointed at his head. "I've got it all tucked right up here, and that's bad enough. Seeing it in print would surely give me a headache."

"So, what are we going to do with that?" Emma asked, pointing at the painting.

"Keep in the living room for a while, I guess," Jennifer replied. "And when we get tired of looking at it, I'll stick it in a closet."

Emma was about to respond when the sheriff arrived at the back door, looking weary and disheveled.

"Well, this is a surprise," Emma said, ushering him into the kitchen. "Though I must say, you look about dead on your feet. Sit down, and I'll get you some tea."

Sheriff Jim Cody had been the sheriff for years, and Jennifer couldn't remember a time when he'd looked so frazzled. He was a large, portly man, who always had a quick, easy smile, but he wasn't smiling now.

"Wes, Jennifer," he said, dropping into a chair. "I'm on my way home, but thought I'd better stop by and give you the news. We've got funny money turning up all over town, and I have to tell you, it has me deeply concerned."

Wes frowned. "Funny money. You mean counterfeit money?"

"That's right. So far we've had only tens, but as I understand it, after talking to a Treasury agent at their field office in Lincoln, the twenty-dollar bills won't be far behind. Seems to be some sort of a pattern. I wouldn't have picked up on it if Ida had found the ten in one of my shirt pockets before she tossed it in the washer last night. Though the printing isn't bad, the ink isn't the best, and runs a bit if it gets wet. So that tells me the counterfeiter isn't a professional. Probably got ahold of some good plates, and is trying to bluff his way through.''

''Lordy, what next!'' Emma said, placing a cup of tea in front of the sheriff.

Wes said, ''So, you have one of the tens. Do you know where you got it?''

''Sure, but that isn't gonna help much. Ida went to the white elephant sale yesterday afternoon. Wanted to get there the first day, figuring to beat the rush. She had two twenty-dollar bills with her. When she stopped by my office on her way home, she had one ten she'd received in change at the sale. I wasn't sure if I was gonna get home for dinner, so she gave me the ten in case I had to get a quick bite at the coffee shop. I stuck it in my pocket, and forgot about it. As it turned out, Nettie brought in a bag of sandwiches from the deli about five, so the ten spot never left my pocket.''

''Who gave Ida the ten?'' Jennifer asked.

''Penelope Davis, when Ida bought a ceramic pig for three dollars. Her change was the ten, a five, and two dollar bills. She spent the seven dollars at some other table, and that left her with the ten. Now, I don't think for one minute Penelope Davis is passing funny money, which means she got it from somebody else. And that's exactly what's gonna make this one difficult case to crack, if it's even possible. The counterfeiter was smart. He knew this would be the perfect time to start this sort of thing. The town is full of tourists, and everybody is spending money. I talked to Penelope this morning, without letting her know what was going on. I just casually asked her about the customers she had before Ida got there. She said her table had been open about an hour, and most of the customers were tourists. Big help, huh? I could catch the counterfeiter passing a phony bill, and I wouldn't be able to prove he was the culprit, because all he'd have to say is that he got it as change from somebody else. I spent most of the day looking at ten-dollar bills, and after a while, I didn't have to give them the water test. I got so I could spot them right off. And I found them all over town. The coffee shop alone had three. It's pretty lucrative when you think about it. The culprit goes into the coffee shop and buys a cup of coffee with a counterfeit ten-dollar bill, and gets back nine dollars and some change in good money. Realistically, he could hit stores all over town in an hour's time, and make a pretty healthy profit.''

"So what else did the Treasury agent say?" Wes asked.

The sheriff sighed. "Not much. He said they'd get to it as soon as they could, acted like it was small potatoes, and suggested I put the whole town on red alert, so no more of the funny stuff can be passed. I tried to tell him we're in the middle of a humongous Labor Day celebration, and the town is full of tourists, but he didn't seem too impressed. Just said that was all the more reason to alert the town. I know I should, and probably will, but that will almost guarantee the counterfeiter will move on, and if we don't catch him, businesses, residents, and tourists alike are in for one big loss. Not to mention how many tourists we'll lose in the process. I can also see everybody demanding the town make good the losses, and I don't have to tell you what that could mean. As it is, I've given receipts to all the places where I've picked up the bogus bills, and it's adding up. I'm at three hundred dollars, and counting."

Emma reached in the cupboard and brought out a jar. "This is where I keep the grocery money, Sheriff. You'll find a couple of tens, and one of them came from the market this afternoon."

The sheriff examined the roll of bills, and

shook his head. "No funny money here, Emma."

Emma let out an audible sigh, and returned the jar to the cupboard.

"I gave Irene Copeland two tens today when I bought that," Jennifer said, pointing at the painting. "But I couldn't begin to tell you where I got them. I cashed a check at the bank last Friday. It was all in twenties, and I've received a lot of tens in change in the interim, which I proceeded to spend here and there. Gas and oil at the gas station, lunch at Kelly's, a pair of shoes at the shoe store, odds and ends at the Mercantile, stamps at the post office, and UPS, who delivered the trophies and ribbons for the dog show, just to name a few."

"And *that*," the sheriff said, scowling at the painting. "Wonder who donated it?"

"Elmer Dodd," Jennifer replied. "I know, don't say it. Whatever I spent, it was too much."

"Well, it's better than some of the other stuff he's donated. Ida bought a candy dish shaped like an upside-down umbrella that was supposed to be an antique, but the sticker on the bottom said 'made in China.' Come to find out, the Mercantile has been selling the same candy dish for the last five years for a buck thirty-five, plus tax."

"Have you talked with the bank?" Wes asked. "I would think that would be the best place to start."

"I already did. They found four tens. I'll also be turning the counterfeit money over to them for safekeeping. What about the clinic, Jennifer? Jennifer?"

Jennifer blinked. "I'm sorry, I was just thinking about something, and I can't seem to get it out of my mind. It happened at the park today. When I got there, Irene was trying to sell a copper teapot to an elderly couple for a dollar fifty, and they thought it was too much. Then Paul came. . . ." When the sheriff raised a brow, she explained briefly, and then went on. "And then Paul came, and somehow, the subject of the teapot came up. A few minutes later, Paul managed to sell the teapot to a young couple for ten dollars, thanks to a lot of smooth talking. And that's when Paul announced he couldn't stay. But before he left, he pulled out a twenty-dollar bill, and asked Irene if she would mind giving him two tens in exchange. She gave him the tens, and he hurried off. It seemed purely innocent at the time, but now that we have a counterfeiter passing ten-dollar bills around town, and if he hadn't acted so strange . . ."

Emma snorted. "So, the man goes from 'knocking your socks off' to being the prime suspect in a matter of minutes. I don't know, Jennifer. That doesn't seem very likely to me. Counterfeiters pass money around, they don't take it back.''

Wes sighed. ''I have the feeling before this is over, everybody is going to be a suspect, Emma, and it's a sad state of affairs.''

Jennifer felt a chill. ''No, counterfeiters don't take the bills they are passing around back, but what if the twenty Paul gave Irene was bogus? The treasury agent said twenty-dollar bills wouldn't be far behind. What if Irene and I actually witnessed the culprit in action?''

A smile tugged at the corners of the sheriff's mouth. ''Well, that's loyalty for you. Love him today, arrest him tomorrow. Just teasing, Jennifer, but right about now, I don't think we can leave anything to chance. No matter what, Paul Bishop is a stranger, and shouldn't be counted out, just because he's tall, handsome, and has a nice doggy. How did he pay you for services rendered at the clinic?''

''I charged him a normal office visit, and a very small fee for cleaning Casey's teeth. The bill came to twenty-eight dollars, and he gave me a twenty, a five, and three ones.''

''What about your other patients this morning?''

"It was a busy morning. Some paid by check, some cash, a few we put on the books."

"Any other twenties?"

"I don't know. Ben counted the receipts, and put it in an envelope."

Wes said, "And is the envelope still in the safe at the clinic?"

Jennifer pulled the envelope out of her purse. "No, it's right here. I was going to make a deposit at the bank this afternoon, but then, when things got so hectic, I decided to wait until tomorrow."

Jennifer opened the envelope, pulled out the contents, and handed three twenties to the sheriff. "Now what?" she said, barely above a whisper.

The sheriff frowned. "I haven't seen any of the bogus twenties, so we'd better try the water test."

A few minutes later, Wes pointed at the smeared twenty-dollar bill, and said, "Bingo!"

With her heart pounding in her throat, Jennifer said, "But is that the twenty Paul gave me? Or did I get it from somebody else?"

"Who came in this morning?" Wes asked.

"Mrs. Wiggs and Sir Scuffy. I'm not sure how she paid, because Ben handled it. Dan Wise and Einstein. He paid by check. Mrs. Thurman and Fancy Dancer. Her check is right here. Oh, and the Cramers' cat, and we had two minor emergency walk-ins. Ben handled those.''

Emma was shaking her head. ''It doesn't matter. You have no way of knowing who gave you that twenty, and even if you could figure it out, they could've gotten it from somebody else.''

''Who is taking care of the proceeds from the white elephant sale?'' Wes asked.

The sheriff replied, ''One of my deputies goes by just before they close at five, collects the money and paperwork, and takes it to City Hall.''

Wes looked at his watch. ''Well, it's too late to check on that now.''

The sheriff nodded. ''But it isn't too late to do some sleuthing.'' He leaned back and drummed his beefy fingers on the table. ''This Paul Bishop. You plan on seeing him again, Jennifer?''

Her reply was succinct. ''No, I don't.''

''Uh-huh, well, you think maybe you might reconsider? You're the best candidate to keep an eye on him. In the interim, you could get some additional information on him, and—''

''Under the circumstances, I think I'd be a very bad candidate,'' Jennifer interrupted.

''Why? Because you're attracted to him? Come on, Jennifer. You just met the man. Besides, you're good at this sort of thing, and I could really use your help.''

The sheriff didn't understand, but then how could she expect him to, when she didn't understand it herself? ''I don't know,'' Jennifer said. ''I might not run into him again. Maybe he's left town.''

Emma snorted. ''I think you're asking too much of Jennifer, Sheriff Cody. She has a busy schedule. Much too busy to have to spend time tracking Paul Bishop all over town.''

Wes reached across the table and squeezed Jennifer's hand. ''Let's leave it up to Jennifer, Jim.''

Feeling as though she were running out of options, Jennifer sighed. ''If I happen to see Paul, I'll do what I can, but I can't promise more than that.''

The sheriff got up and stretched. ''Fair enough. Guess I'd better be on my way. Ida is expecting me home for supper, and she isn't in a good mood. I'll let you know what I decide in the morning, Wes. With only eight deputies trying to cover everything that's going on, if I do decide to make an official announcement, I'll need some dependable help.'' He smiled at Emma. ''Thanks for the tea, Emma, and be sure and save me one of your jars of strawberry jam. I'd ask you to save me a slice of apple pie, too, but Ida is entering a pie in the apple pie contest this year, and I sure don't want to create any waves. My life is rocky enough. See you all tomorrow.''

After the sheriff left, Jennifer went upstairs to freshen up, but her thoughts were on Paul Bishop, and they were confusing at best. A part of her prayed he'd already left town, a part of her wanted to help the sheriff, and yet there was also a tiny part of her that wanted to see him again, and that was the hardest thing of all to accept.

Chapter Three

Because nearly half of Calico's residents were involved in the Labor Day festivities in some way, and with most of them in total disagreement about how things should be run, Jennifer drove to the Grange the following morning prepared for total chaos. It happened every year to some degree, but this year it was worse, because the town council had decided to take an active part in the preparations, and they never agreed on anything, either. A good example of that had been at the last town meeting, when the crotchety old men—led by Mayor Attwater—had spent two hours arguing over who was going to judge the cooking contests. As far as Jennifer knew, it still wasn't settled, though they were strongly leaning toward using their own wives. Emma had been outraged at just the *thought* of it, and with good reason, because most of the wives, who were crotchety old women, were planning to enter the cooking contests, too, so how could that possibly be equitable?

There had also been a heated debate on whether campaign banners and posters should be displayed around the fairgrounds, until Willy stood up and announced that he didn't think the fair was the appropriate place to try to garner votes, and as far as he was concerned, the mayoral race should be put on hold until after the holiday. Elmer had come back at Willy, calling him a hick attorney who didn't know the first thing about campaigning, and if Willy hadn't kept his cool and used diplomacy, the situation could have easily gotten out of hand. But, in the end, Willy won the debate, guaranteeing that there wouldn't be any campaign paraphernalia on display at the fairgrounds.

There had been some controversy, too, over how much money the residents should spend at the arts and crafts show, with the mayor reminding everybody that even though each of the vendors had to pay a healthy fee to buy space at the fair, every dollar they collected in sales would stay in their pockets. But when he'd suggested a five-dollar limit, and somebody else suggested ten, Rose Kelly, who owned the boardinghouse, jumped up and announced that she worked hard for her money, had every right to spend it the way she wanted, and as far as she was concerned, the mayor was way out of line for even suggesting such a dumb thing. At that point, Elmer Dodd had jumped up, defending the mayor, Willy had jumped up, defending Rose Kelly, and it had taken Wes to bring the meeting to order, by reminding everyone the vendors would be shopping in town during their stay, as well as eating at the restaurants, and businesses could only profit. Things had calmed down after that, but it hadn't been the end of the discord, which had gotten steadily worse as the big week drew closer and closer. Now, hopefully, there would be no time for dissension, because the holiday had arrived, whether they were ready or not.

Jennifer pulled the Jeep into the parking area behind the Grange that had been set aside for the residents who would be working at the fair, and sighed. She had spent a miserable, sleepless night trying to come to terms with what the sheriff wanted her to do, and now she felt headachy and fidgety. Not a good way to begin the day that was destined to be an unorganized muddle at best. And even worse than that, she'd spent a good hour trying to find something appropriate to wear, again, in the event she ran into Paul Bishop. She'd finally settled on white cotton pants, because she wanted to be comfortable, but wasn't sure why she'd chosen the pink, gauzy, off-the-shoulder blouse.

Brought out of her musings when she heard the truck pull in beside her, Jennifer climbed out of the Jeep and smiled. It was Cracker Martin, a wonderful old man who owned a little farm in the foothills, with a view of the valley that went on forever. He had been a widower for several years, and lived with an assortment of pigs, chickens, a cow named Daisy, and Sam, an exuberant Newfoundland Jennifer had given him last Christmas, to replace his beloved St. Bernard.

Cracker was wearing his typical blue jeans, plaid shirt, and colorful suspenders, and, also typically, his gray hair was standing on end.

"Hi, Cracker," Jennifer said, kissing his weathered cheek. "Are you working at the fair today?"

His smile was warm, and his dark eyes twinkled. "That I am, young lady. I'm workin' the baseball booth from nine until ten, the dart booth from ten-thirty till eleven-thirty, and then I'm officiatin' over the sack race. They wanted me to be an umpire for one of the softball games this afternoon, but my back couldn't take it. It

ain't what it used to be. Left Sam home, too.
Figured as big as he is, he'd just be in the way,
and didn't think he'd take too kindly to all the
confusion. Figured he'd be a lot better off
watching over the pigs, and chickens, and Daisy
Cow. What about you? They got you working
from dawn to dusk?''

"Actually, my schedule isn't too bad. I got
off easy, because I have to spend so many hours
at the dog show on Sunday. I work the bake sale
for an hour this morning, and then two hours at
the petting zoo this afternoon. The rest of the
time, I'll be filling in where I'm needed."

"You and Ben are the judges for that dog
show, huh?''

"Yes, we are, and you really should enter
Sam. I can almost guarantee you he'd win a ribbon for the largest dog, even though he's still
considered a puppy. One hundred pounds, and
growing.''

Cracker shrugged. "I thought about it, but I
don't know nothin' about dog shows, 'cept what
I see on TV. Sounds pretty highfalutin to me.''

"It isn't going to be like a normal AKC dog
show, Cracker. It doesn't matter if the dogs are
pedigreed or not, or what they look like, or how
well they behave in the ring. We're going to
give out ribbons and trophies for the largest dog,

the smallest dog, the tallest dog, the fattest dog, and the shaggiest dog—that sort of thing.''

They were making their way between the cars, and Jennifer slowed her pace. A dark-green panel van with a New York license plate was parked under a shady tree directly in front of them.

When Cracker realized Jennifer was lagging behind, he turned around, caught her expression, and frowned. ''You've got a mighty strange look on your face, young lady.''

Jennifer managed a smile for Cracker's benefit. ''That van doesn't belong in the residents' parking area, that's all.''

Cracker looked at the van, and squinted. ''From New York. No, it sure don't, unless it belongs to a relative of one of Calico's citizens. I've heard that kinfolk are showin' up from just about every corner of the state, and a few have even come across country, just to share in the festivities. Well, I say their money is just as good as anybody's, and I hope they open their wallets wide. Uh-huh, well, whoever owns that van has some money to spend. Custom wheels and paint job, if you ask me. And you see that antenna? That means they've got one of those fancy car phones.'' He peered through the closed driver's window. ''Custom seats, too. Can't see in the back, but I'll bet it's got all the comforts of home. Maybe even more. Saw the inside of a vehicle like this once, and it was really something. Even had a TV.''

Fully expecting Paul Bishop to pop out of the bushes or from behind a tree, and catch them looking at the van, Jennifer moved on, calling over her shoulder, ''Come on, Cracker. It's getting late. We'd better hurry if you're supposed to start work at nine.''

Cracker caught up with her and grinned. ''So what if I'm a few minutes late? What are they gonna do, fire me? So where's your grandpa and Emma?''

''Emma is coming along later with a neighbor, but she'll be here in plenty of time for the pie and jam judging. And Grandfather had a breakfast meeting. They still have a lot of plans to make for the barbecue on Monday. They expect a large turnout, so they might have to build a few extra barbecue pits.''

''Well, I guess we should all be mighty thankful the greenbelt along the river wasn't washed away in the flood.''

''I know,'' Jennifer replied. ''We have a lot to be thankful for. . . .'' Her words trailed off as she caught sight of the tall blond man in the white pants and blue shirt standing near the concession stand. He was drinking a cup of coffee with one hand, holding Casey's leash with the other, and gazing off toward the Grange. He didn't see her, and she lowered her voice. ''I have to talk to that man over there, Cracker, so I'll catch you later, okay?''

Cracker raised a brow, but didn't comment, and Jennifer was eternally grateful.

Though it was early, and the crowd was still small, the atmosphere was already festive, with high-flying banners and balloons, brightly decorated booths, and the sound of children laughing at the far end of the grounds, where games were already under way.

Barbara Thurman, Judge Thurman's wife, was working the concession stand with two teenagers, but they were so busy making cotton candy, Barbara didn't see Jennifer as she slipped by. Grateful for that, too, though she knew before the day was over, she would probably get bombarded with questions regarding one Paul Bishop, she took a deep breath, and walked up to the man.

Casey greeted her with wiggles and yips, and she gave him a hug. ''It's good to see you, too, Casey.'' She looked up at Paul, felt some funny things happen to her insides, and said, ''I didn't expect to see you here today.''

He grinned, the dimple flashed, and he drawled, ''I don't know why not. It's opening day, and this is what it's all about.''

"Well, after yesterday, I thought you might be on your way home."

A muscle worked along his jawline. "Because something came up unexpectedly and I had to leave? I'm genuinely sorry about that, Jennifer. If you'll let me, I'd like to make it up to you. Hot dogs and sodas at high noon, right here. Deal?"

"It depends on my schedule," she said quickly, and then just as quickly, she remembered what the sheriff wanted her to do, and nodded. "Hot dogs and sodas at noon."

His blue eyes twinkled, and they were the color of the sky. "Good! May I buy you a cup of coffee?"

"No, but you can walk with me. I have to talk to the mayor, who is coordinating things, and check my schedule."

"So, you're working this morning?"

"At the bake sale from ten until eleven."

Paul looked at his watch. "So that gives us an hour to make up for our lost hour yesterday. What happens from eleven to twelve?"

"I'll fill in if I'm needed anywhere. If I'm not, I'll watch the pie and jam judging. But I don't have an hour now, Paul. Sorry."

"Okay, what about this afternoon?"

"I'm scheduled to work at the petting zoo

from two until four. I'll also fill in where needed.''

Paul looked around. ''I don't see the petting zoo.''

''It's behind the Grange, adjacent to the live-stock exhibition.''

''And tomorrow?''

Aware that he obviously wanted to know where she was going to be at every moment, and knowing it would work to her advantage, too, to be with him as much as possible, Jennifer replied, ''I have a lot of errands to run and things to do to get ready for the dog show on Sunday, but other than that, I'm not scheduled to work at the fair, or the white elephant sale. Sunday I'll be tied up most of the day with the dog show, but I can relax at the barbecue on Monday. We all can.''

Paul said, ''From what I've heard, anybody can go to the barbecue, including the tourists, and that sounds like a monumental undertaking to me.''

''Yes, but we're holding it on the greenbelt along the river where there is plenty of room, and everybody will have to buy a food ticket to attend, so it's really a good way of making money. And it won't be so bad. My grandfather is in charge, and he has an impressive, hard-working committee. He's at a meeting this morning, finalizing the plans. And they are going to keep it simple. Barbecued ribs and hot dogs, corn on the cob, salads, and watermelon.''

''I've heard Nebraska's soil is pretty good for growing watermelons.''

''It's the best. They'll also use large wading pools filled with ice to keep the cans of soda cold.''

Paul tossed the Styrofoam coffee cup in a trash receptacle, and cleared his throat. ''What about the dance at the pavilion on Saturday night?''

Jennifer knew what was coming, but didn't know how to respond. She'd planned to go to the dance with Ken Hering, and she didn't see how she could possibly get out of it without causing ill feelings, unless she told Ken the truth. But she didn't want to do that, until she talked to the sheriff.

Finally, she said, ''What about it?''

''I guess I just wanted to know if you're going, and that's a dumb question. You're a pretty lady, and you probably have a dozen guys beating down your door.''

His comment brought a smile to Jennifer's face. ''Nobody is 'beating down my door,' Paul, and I'd like to go to the dance, but I can't give you an answer right now, if you're asking me to go with you.''

"Guess that was pretty obvious, huh? So, will you think about it?"

"I'll think about it, promise."

They had reached the small trailer that had been brought in to use as an office, and Jennifer smiled up at Paul. "Hot dogs and sodas at noon, right?"

Paul nodded and walked off, but not before she'd seen the disappointment on his face. And she knew how he felt, even though admitting it wasn't easy. It was going to be a long three hours for her, as well.

Surprised to see only Elmer Dodd and the sheriff in the trailer, Jennifer sat down at the table and asked, "Where are the mayor and the town council?"

Elmer Dodd, a short, plump man with dark hair and beady eyes, who was wearing his usual white suit and black string tie, puffed out his cheeks. "The mayor is ailing, and the rest of them had other things to do, so I guess that puts me in charge." He looked at the sheriff. "I suppose you told her all about our problem?"

"She knows," the sheriff said. "Good morning, Jennifer. Hope you had a better night than I did. Spent half of it trying to decide what to do about our latest predicament, and the other half trying to figure out how to catch the culprit. First dilemma sort of solved itself this morning, when Lester at the bank called at daybreak, and said he'd gotten in several hundred dollars' worth of tens and twenties, all brought in yesterday from businesses in their daily receipts. Knew right then and there I was going to have to alert the town. First step is to contact all the businesses, which I'll do this morning. If they receive a ten or a twenty from a customer, the customer will be told they have to either write a check for their purchases, use a credit card or a traveler's check or, if they want to take the time, they can go to the bank or the sheriff's office to have the bills checked out.''

Elmer snorted. ''And I say if the customers have to go through that rigmarole, they won't bother. Before you know it, everybody will be pulling out.''

Sheriff Cody frowned. ''Unless you have a better suggestion, Dodd, it's the only way. I could have all the businesses accept the tens and twenties and put them all aside for verification, but what then? If any of it is funny money, the customer who passed it will be long gone with his purchase, the business will be out the money, and it will continue on, like a creeping virus. This is the only way to stop it, disgruntled customers or not. We're alerting everybody who is working at the fair and handling money, too, and that includes the arts and crafts people. Put simply, nobody will be able to accept any tens or twenties.

"I talked to John Wexler over at *The Calico Review* first thing this morning, and he'll make an announcement in the morning paper. That way, if we overlook somebody who should be notified, they'll be put on alert through the paper."

"I say we should keep quiet about the whole thing until the fair is over," Elmer said heatedly. "Publicity like this is going to kill us."

The sheriff scowled at the man. "You ever see the movie *Jaws*? If I recall, a small seaside town was having a big holiday celebration of some sort, and when a man-eating shark was discovered lurking in the water, the town fathers kept it quiet for fear all the tourists would run off. So what happens? A bunch of people got killed."

Elmer returned his scowl. "You're talking about fiction, Sheriff, and it's hardly the same thing. We're not talking about people dying here."

"Maybe not, but financially, it could be pretty darned disastrous."

"So, do you have a plan to catch the counterfeiter?" Jennifer asked.

The sheriff shook his head. "Unless we can find somebody with the plates, and that sure isn't likely, I don't think we have a chance, Jennifer. That was my second dilemma, and it's still a dilemma. I think the counterfeiter is making the bogus bills in some other town, Anytown USA, and then takes the bills out and around until he runs out, and then goes back to home base to replenish his supply. And that's pretty imposing when you think about it. What if a whole bunch of people are involved? Think about how many towns a network like that could cover at one time. I'm convinced all we can do at this point is alert the town to keep the stuff off the streets, and wait for the Feds. Meanwhile, the fair goes on, and we try to have a good time.''

Jennifer looked at her watch. ''I have to get to the bake sale. Does anybody know where the mayor put the schedule? I'd like to check it before I get started.''

Elmer Dodd pursed his lips. ''Hey, if you can find it, you let me know. I called Mayor Attwater. He said it was in that drawer over there, but it isn't, and I can't find it anywhere.''

Jennifer sighed. ''Well, let's hope everybody knows what they're supposed to be doing, and when.''

''Let's hope,'' the sheriff said. ''If you're heading over to the bake sale now, Jennifer, I'll walk with you.''

They'd reached the door when Elmer Dodd said, "I understand you bought my painting yesterday, Jennifer. Just want you to know how difficult it was for me to part with it. It was one of my daddy's favorites, and I let it go for a song. The frame alone is worth big bucks."

Jennifer thought about the "made in China" candy dish Ida had purchased, supposedly from the dregs of Elmer's basement, and walked out without commenting, but she caught the expression on the sheriff's face. He was biting his tongue, too.

"Jerk," the sheriff said, after they were outside. He took a deep breath. "I could tell you wanted to talk to me alone, Jennifer. Knew it the minute you walked in."

"Well, part of what I wanted to talk to you about has already been answered, Sheriff. Paul Bishop asked me to go to the dance with him tomorrow night. I planned to go with Ken, but in light of what you want me to do . . . I was afraid if I broke the date with Ken it would cause hard feelings, but now that you've already talked to John, Jr., and you're alerting the town, I'll be able to tell Ken the truth. Hopefully, he'll understand."

The sheriff raised a brow. "When did you see Paul Bishop?"

"He was already here when I got here this

morning, Sheriff Cody. We're going to meet for lunch.''

The sheriff nodded. ''Well, that's a start. Not that I really think the man is our counterfeiter, you understand, but like I said last night, he can't be counted out. Guess nobody can be, and that's the rotten part of it. I keep thinking, if the Cromwell sisters can make moonshine in their bathtub, maybe Calico has its own homegrown counterfeiter. I remember reading about an old lady one time, who had a counterfeiting plate. She didn't know the first thing about printing funny money, and used green food coloring in an old washing machine for the dye job. With disastrous results, I might add. Wonder if that's the way 'laundering money' got its name?'' He grinned at Jennifer. ''Just a stab at humor in this trying time. So, you're meeting Paul Bishop for lunch, and he's taking you to the dance tomorrow night.''

''I haven't said I'll go, but I probably will. . . . You're not insinuating that the Cromwell sisters have figured out a way to make counterfeit money, are you?''

The sheriff shook his head. ''No way, Jennifer. I know, their papa and uncle were bootleggers back in Prohibition, but the sisters are harmless. They don't sell their hooch, they use it for 'medicinal' purposes, and that's why I look the other way.''

They had reached the bake sale booth, and he breathed in deeply. ''Smells even better than it looks, but I sure don't need the calories. You keep me posted, you hear? And if anything important happens, I'll be in my office later this afternoon.''

Jennifer said she would call him if she had anything to report, but her thoughts were on the dance at the pavilion, and dancing under the stars in Paul Bishop's arms. . . .

Chapter Four

"How about a picture of you eating that hot dog dripping with mustard," Ken Hering said, joining Jennifer at one of the picnic tables near the concession stand. He placed the camera on the table, and made a square with his hands. "Caption: PRETTY VET ENJOYING HERSELF AT THE FAIR."

Jennifer wiped her mouth, and managed a smile. "That would hardly be a newsworthy event for the morning paper, Ken."

"I'm not out shooting 'newsworthy' photos, Jennifer. It's human-interest stuff all the way, like Ben Copeland in the dunk tank, the watermelon eating contest, Emma holding up her blue ribbons, Judge Thurman sliding into third base

72

at the softball game, two old ladies in a shouting match, Rose Kelly getting soaked with a water balloon, and . . .'' His green eyes narrowed over her. ''Earth to Jennifer.''

Jennifer blinked, and looked at the redheaded reporter. ''Sorry. What were you saying?''

''That's not important. What *is* important is the reason for the glum expression on your face and that faraway look in your eyes. Do I dare venture a guess? It's that blond jerk with the blond dog, isn't it?''

Jennifer took a deep breath. ''Who told you about Paul?''

''The sheriff. He told me what you're doing. When I said I didn't like it, he said now wasn't the time for me to get jealous, and I said it didn't have a cotton-picking thing to do with jealousy. If Paul Bishop is our counterfeiter, he could be dangerous, and that makes me nervous.''

''Your concern would be put to better use someplace else,'' Jennifer muttered. ''I can hardly be in danger when the man is never around. We had a lunch date yesterday that he couldn't keep, and I was supposed to meet him here today for lunch, and he stood me up. I haven't seen him since early this morning, so I can only assume he's no longer on the fairgrounds.''

''Now I *know* he's a jerk. Well, from what I

understand, he wouldn't be hard to miss, so if you say he isn't here, he probably isn't here. I talked to Tina earlier, and it was Paul Bishop this, and Paul Bishop that. She said he spent an hour with her at the petting zoo this morning, and apparently, it was enough time for her to fall in love with him. I won't go into all the things she said about him, but I got the message.''

''She fell in love with him when he walked into the clinic yesterday morning, Ken. But you know how girls can be at that age.''

''Uh-huh, well, I know how girls can be at any age when a tall, handsome man is involved. Especially a tall, handsome stranger who is a bit of a mystery.''

As far as Jennifer was concerned, the only mystery involved here was why Paul had spent an hour at the petting zoo with Tina, when he hadn't come by the bake sale at all, and why he hadn't shown up for lunch, when it had been his idea in the first place. But she knew what Ken was getting at. He wanted to know how she *really* felt about the tall, handsome stranger, and if he should be concerned on a personal level.

She reached across the table, and squeezed Ken's hand. ''Paul Bishop will only be here for a couple of days, Ken. He's simply passing through, on his way to South Dakota.''

"Uh-huh, and I say it's a good thing. I suppose you want to break our date so you can go to the dance with him? All in the name of keeping him under surveillance, of course."

Jennifer sighed. "I'll admit he asked me, and I'll admit I was considering it, but his little stunt today really made me angry. So, I won't be going to the dance with him, and as far as I'm concerned, if the sheriff wants to find out more about the man, he can do it!"

"So, does that mean we're on again for the dance?"

"We were never really off, Ken, and I'm truly sorry for even considering it. You're a good friend, and . . ."

"Hi, you two," Tina said, plopping down at the table. "Hope I'm not interrupting anything important, but I'm just so excited, I could explode! Tony Sugarman wants to take me to the dance tomorrow night."

Jennifer raised a brow. "Tony Sugarman?"

Ken shook his head. "Well, if this is gonna be girl talk, I'm out of here." He leaned over and kissed Jennifer's cheek. I'll pick you up around seven tomorrow night. Okay?"

"I'll be ready," Jennifer said, trying for a smile.

Tina watched Ken walk away, and frowned.

"I thought you were going to the dance with Paul."

"Did he tell you that?"

"In so many words."

"Well, it was never confirmed, one way or the other, so I would say that was pretty presumptuous of him, and that's what I'm going to tell him, *if* I ever have the misfortune of seeing him again."

Tina's frown deepened. "You sound really angry, Jennifer."

"I *am* really angry, but I don't want to get into it now. So, who is Tony Sugarman?"

Tina's eyes twinkled. "Just about the most gorgeous guy I've ever seen. . . . Well, maybe not quite as gorgeous as Paul Bishop, but Tony is pretty terrific. Dark hair and eyes, a great smile, and he wears the neatest cowboy shirts. He and his dad are vendors at the arts and crafts show. They tool leather. You know, wallets, belts, boots, that sort of thing, and do beautiful work."

Jennifer remembered seeing the two cowboy types tooling leather in a corner booth when she'd been in the Grange earlier, but she hadn't paid much attention to them. She'd been much more interested in the lovely ceramics made by a couple from New Mexico, and the various jewelry booths, displaying everything from California jade to opals from Australia. "How old is Tony Sugarman?" Jennifer asked finally.

Tina shrugged. "Maybe twenty or twenty-one."

"And how do you think your parents are going to feel about that? He's older. He's a stranger, and . . ."

Tina waved a hand. "I didn't say I'm going to go with him, but I thought it was really cool he asked. I'll probably see him there, but that's okay, 'cause Mom and Dad are going to the dance, and I'll be with a group of friends. Well, I *guess* I'll see him there. His dad was pretty mad at him for staying away from their booth so long. He spent nearly an hour with me at the petting zoo, when he was only supposed to be taking a ten-minute break."

"Sounds like your morning was filled with long-winded visitors. Ken told me Paul Bishop was there for almost an hour, too."

Tina's face brightened. "Yeah, he was, and he was so good with the animals. He even got Mr. Babkins's peacock to eat out of his hand, and you *know* how temperamental that old bird can be. He's fine with kids, but the adults better watch out."

"You worked at the petting zoo for two hours this morning," Jennifer said, popping the last of the hot dog in her mouth. "So, did Paul come by the first hour? Or the second?"

"Actually, they sort of overlapped. Why?"

"I'd like to know where Paul was shortly before lunch, that's all. He was supposed to meet me here at noon, but he stood me up."

"Well, that's sure strange, because he said he was meeting you for lunch, and seemed really pleased. When I said they sort of overlapped, I meant that Tony came to the petting zoo first. He was there about a half hour when Paul came. They were there together about a half hour, and then Tony left."

"Do you have any idea what time Paul left?"

Tina scrunched her brows in thought. "Probably about a quarter to twelve."

"And which way was he headed?"

"Toward the residents' parking area. Boy, that seems strange, too, because if he was meeting you for lunch in a few minutes, why would he head for the parking area? And why the residents' parking area?"

"Because he parked his van there, Tina. I saw it on my way in this morning. Do you remember what he talked about during that hour he was with you?"

"He didn't have much to say during the first half hour, because Tony was doing all the talking. Then after Tony left, he talked about the town, mostly. He wanted to know where the proceeds from the fair were being kept, that sort of thing.''

Jennifer felt a chill. ''Didn't you think that was strange?''

''Not really, because Tony asked me the same thing. And earlier, I heard Cracker Martin talking to Penelope Davis about it. What with all the funny money floating around town, it's on everybody's mind.'' Tina stood up. ''Gotta go. The fair closes in an hour, and I'm on the cleanup committee. I probably won't see you tomorrow, 'cause my mom wants me to do some stuff around the house, but I'll see you tomorrow night.''

With the thought of dancing under the stars with Paul now nothing more than a painful memory, Jennifer nodded wearily, and headed for the Jeep. It was time to go home, where everything was right and wonderful, and maybe she could forget.

Emma was the one who finally put the whole thing into perspective later that night. They were sitting out on the porch like they did almost every summer evening, drinking tall glasses of iced tea while fireflies lit up the dark velvet sky, and the scent of honeysuckle wafted through the air. Emma and Wes knew Jennifer was troubled, and why, but had kept from commenting until now, when they could share this special time and take solace from the peace and tranquillity around them.

They had been discussing the events of the day when Emma cleared her throat, and said, "I can understand your disappointment, honey. He's a handsome man and you are attracted to him, but don't forget, you hardly know him, and from his behavior, I'd say it's a good thing. He's obviously the undependable sort, and Lord only knows what else. Take comfort in the fact he'll be leaving in a few days, and that it could have been oh so much worse."

Wes said, "I think Emma means you could've fallen in love with him, sweetheart, and that truly would've been a sad state of affairs."

Jennifer sighed. "So my heart was only broken a little bit instead of a lot, but that doesn't stop this overwhelming feeling of anger that I can't seem to shake. And if he's the counterfeiter, it's even worse, because he hasn't just duped me, he's duped the whole town."

"And I'd say he just might get away with it," Wes said. "Unless the federal authorities come in with a plan, the sheriff's hands are tied. He's done all he can, but at least he was able to get the counterfeit money off the street. I talked to him before I came home, and he was pleased to say almost everybody has cooperated and seems to understand, and that includes most of the tourists. Because of it, it was a day without incident.''

Emma pursed her lips. ''If Paul Bishop is the culprit, maybe that's why he took off in such a hurry. Maybe he knew his business in Calico had come to an end. You said after Tina talked to him, he headed for the parking area. Maybe he left town.''

''Did you see him at the fair, Emma?'' Jennifer asked. ''I realize you don't know the man, but you could hardly miss him going by my description.''

''I did. It was a few minutes before the pie judging. I went around behind the judges' table to get my apron, and saw him talking to a pretty blond lady wearing a red flowered dress. That would've been around a quarter to eleven.''

''That sounds like Julia Colby. She and her husband are from New Mexico, and they make wonderful Southwest-style ceramics.''

Emma harrumphed. ''Well, her husband wasn't with them, and their conversation looked pretty intense.''

''Did he have Casey with him?'' Jennifer asked.

''He did. Casey was sitting there at the man's

feet, like the most well-behaved dog in the world.''

Wes grinned. ''On a more pleasant note, congratulations again for winning two blue ribbons, Emma. That ought to prove to everybody that you make the best strawberry jam and apple pies in town.''

Emma snorted. ''Wouldn't have won a consolation prize if the town fathers had put their wives to judging. Lordy, that would've been the ticket.''

''So who ended up judging?'' Wes asked.

''Frances Cromwell, Nora Muller, Orris Ford, and Judge Thurman. Fanny was supposed to judge, but she wasn't feeling well, and stayed home.''

Jennifer frowned. ''You mentioned Fanny wasn't feeling well before, Emma. Did Frances say what's wrong with her?''

''No, but I got the impression Frances is worried, because she rushed off after the judging. Said she had to get some things at the market for Fanny.''

''I'll go out to the cottage tomorrow and check on them,'' Wes said.

Emma nodded. ''And I'll go with you. I have some free time in the morning.''

''What are you doing tomorrow afternoon?'' Jennifer asked.

Emma smiled coyly. "Getting my hair done for the dance. Guess I forget to tell you, I talked your granddaddy into taking me."

Wes groaned. "I haven't been on a dance floor in ten years. The last time was at a wedding reception when I danced with the bride."

"And I haven't been on a dance floor in twenty years," Emma returned. "So it looks like we can both look forward to getting our toes good and trounced. But it will be so much fun, and now that they've rebuilt the pavilion . . ."

Emma's words trailed off at the sound of footsteps, and then she could only gasp, "What on earth is *he* doing here?"

It was Elmer Dodd, wearing his infamous white suit and carrying his Panama hat. And he looked terrible! Eyes hollow, face pale, and every breath was a wheeze.

"Well, good evening, Elmer," Wes said, standing up to shake the man's hand. "Sit a spell and have some tea. You sure look like you could use a glass."

Elmer settled into one of the white wicker chairs, and mopped his brow with a handkerchief. "I could surely use something cold," he said, trying to catch his breath.

Wes handed him a glass. "We don't use much sugar around here, so if it's too tart . . ."

"No, this is fine." He looked at Jennifer.

''I've come to buy back that painting you bought, Jennifer. I'll give you fifty dollars. That's a profit of twenty-five. I realize now I shouldn't have given it to the white elephant sale. It's been in my family for years, and it was one of my daddy's favorite paintings.''

Jennifer was going to tell him that if it was that important, she would sell it back to him for what she paid for it, but Wes spoke up first. ''I thought you said you hated that painting, and couldn't wait to get rid of it.''

Elmer's beady eyes lowered. ''Got it mixed up with another painting. ''I'll give you a hundred dollars, Jennifer. Two hundred. Just name your price.''

''I think we should talk about this,'' Wes said. ''Jennifer happens to like that painting, and I know for a fact you don't, no matter what kind of malarkey you're trying to hand us now. I distinctly remember the day you told me the painting of the eagle was the worst piece of artwork in your house, and if you had your way, you'd use it for firewood. That was before your daddy died, of course. As I recall, he had it hanging above the fireplace in his bedroom. After he died, you took it down to the basement, where I'm sure it's been ever since.''

Ignoring Wes's comments, Elmer said shakily, ''I said name your price, Jennifer.''

Baffled by Elmer's behavior, but more intrigued by her grandfather's attitude, Jennifer said, "I'm sorry, Mr. Dodd. The painting isn't for sale at any price."

Elmer jumped up and shouted, "You can't do that! That's *my* painting!"

Emma snorted. "I'd say it's Jennifer's painting now. She came by it fair and square, and she paid a good price. Much too much, if you ask me. Didn't you see the sign on each table? All sales are final, no exchanges or refunds."

Elmer loosened his shirt collar, and looked at Jennifer imploringly. "Will you at least *think* about it?"

Jennifer nodded. "I'll think about it, but I can't make any promises."

After Elmer plodded off, Emma clucked her tongue. "What on earth do you make of that?"

Wes said, "I'd say he's found out the painting is worth big money, and his loss is Jennifer's gain."

Emma reasoned, "But how could he have found that out after the fact? An art dealer would know if he could look at the painting, but we don't have an art dealer in Calico, and Elmer no longer has the painting."

"He seemed so desperate, I really wanted to give it back to him," Jennifer said. "But I thought I'd better play along, even if I don't understand any of it.''

"And I'm not saying you won't give it back to him in the end," Wes said. "But let's wait and see what happens."

"I could never take more than I paid for it, no matter what it's worth."

"I know you couldn't, sweetheart, and I wouldn't want you to. But there is something about this whole thing that isn't sitting well. I suggest we wait until after the fair, and then decide what we're going to do."

"Won't hurt him one bit to stew," Emma said. "It'll give him something else to do besides think about the campaign, and all the underhanded things he's planning to do to Willy before the election."

Jennifer nodded, but she was thinking about the painting, and the real reason Elmer Dodd wanted it back. It wasn't that he liked it, and it simply couldn't be the painting itself, but . . . "Maybe it's the frame," she said suddenly. "Maybe it really is an antique."

Emma smiled. "You see that, Wes? If nothing else, Elmer Dodd piqued Jennifer's interest, and now *she's* got something else to think about besides Paul Bishop."

"Paul Bishop? Who's he?" Jennifer asked a little flippantly. A little *too* flippantly, because in her heart, she knew it was going to take a lot more than the painting and Elmer Dodd's strange behavior to make her forget about Paul Bishop.

Chapter Five

There was no way to adequately describe a dance at the pavilion under a late-summer, star-spangled sky, other than to call it utterly romantic. Rebuilt after the flood had carried a good portion of it down the river, the pavilion was now painted white instead of green, had copious amounts of latticework, and a deck overlooking the river had been added, which was the perfect spot to "sit the next dance out," and watch the lazy, meandering river roll by. Colorful lights and lanterns had been strung everywhere, adding to the festive mood, and the music was being furnished by a group of musicians from North Platte, who were donating their services. The only instructions they'd been given was to play good dance music, to remember the crowd would be a blend of young and old, and their last set was to end at midnight.

At the moment, Jennifer and Ken were on the deck, ''sitting the next dance out,'' drinking punch, and sharing a plate of cookies provided by the refreshment committee.

''Is this where they held the Labor Day dance last year?'' Ken asked, reaching for a lemon wafer.

Jennifer shook her head. ''I keep forgetting you haven't been in Calico all that long. It seems like you've been here forever.''

He gave her a lopsided smile. ''Should I take that as a compliment?''

''It simply means I'm used to having you around, I guess.''

''Then I'll take it as a compliment. I moved to Calico from St. Louis in early October, so I've been here almost a year.''

''Well, last Labor Day, the dance was held at the Grange, and we had a country-western theme.''

''Like a hoedown?''

''Uh-huh, but with a bunch of modern country-western dances thrown in. I learned to do the Texas two-step, the line dance, and the 'Achy Breaky' before it was over.''

''Sounds like fun.''

"It was, but I like this atmosphere better. I also think it was a good idea to have advance ticket sales. It's kept attendance down to a manageable crowd, giving us room to breathe."

"And dance," Ken added. His eyes flickered over her appreciatively. "If I haven't said it before, you look terrific tonight, Jennifer. A pretty pink dress on a very pretty lady. It's quite a combination."

Warmed by his compliment, Jennifer smiled. "That's really sweet, Ken, but you don't look so shabby yourself. Khaki slacks and a brown silk skirt. I didn't know if 'dress casually' would mean you would wear jeans."

Ken nodded at the cowboy vendor, who was talking to Tina at a nearby table. "You mean like that?"

"He probably doesn't have anything but jeans in his wardrobe."

"And 'casual' means different things to different people," Ken said.

"Tell me about it! Emma bought a new flowered dress for the dance, and when she found out Grandfather was going to wear his 'comfortable' old blue slacks, and his 'comfortable' old blue shirt, she had a fit. He finally settled on his new blue slacks and a white shirt and tie to make her happy, but if you'll notice, he's removed his tie."

"Ah, but they look like they're having a good time, and that's really all that matters."

Jennifer watched her grandfather whirl Emma around the floor to the strains of a golden oldie, and sighed. "You'd never know Emma sprained her ankle a few days ago, though I suppose no amount of discomfort would have kept her away from this. She's really been looking forward to it. Though we did have a bit of a setback this morning, and I was afraid they were going to cancel out. They went out to the Cromwell sisters' cottage to check on Fanny, who has been ailing, and found the poor little lady in a great deal of discomfort with a monumental toothache, and not even a couple of glasses of their special 'elixir' could ease the pain. Both ladies need extensive work done on their teeth, but they don't have any insurance, and they simply can't afford it. Grandfather went to the pharmacy straightaway, and bought one of those emergency packs for a toothache, but it's only a temporary remedy. Grandfather and Emma came home terribly upset, and when I came home for lunch, they were trying to figure out a way to help them, so the sisters wouldn't think of it as charity."

"Sounds like one giant task to me, knowing how proud those ladies are. I know they are renting their little cottage out on Marshton Road for a couple of nickels, but does anybody know how they got into their financial straits?''

''I'm surprised John, Jr., hasn't told you.''

Ken shrugged. ''I didn't ask.''

''Well, to make a long story short, Frances and Fanny were raised by their father and his brother, who were bootleggers during Prohibition. After the Cromwell men died, Frances and Fanny kept the old homestead going for quite a few years, and then fell on hard times. The bank foreclosed, and they moved into the cottage.''

''Did they keep the old homestead going by selling hooch?''

''No, they didn't. They were taught how to make the moonshine, but as far as we know, they haven't sold one drop. They give it away, use it for medicinal purposes, and use it in their cooking. To tell you the truth, I don't know what they live on, but they're frugal at best.''

''But they grow vegetables and raise chickens, right?''

''Yes, and they have a cow. I'm sure they also barter a lot. You know, a couple jars of moonshine for a couple of roosters. That sort of thing, which isn't exactly legal, but the sheriff looks the other way.''

''What happened to the old homestead?''

''The bank has been trying to sell it since the

day they foreclosed. It's five acres, but poorly shaped. Narrow at the front and wide at the back. Sort of the shape of a wedge of pie. It also butts up to the east side of the dairy, and who wants to live next to a dairy, and the old house is a falling-down mess. I'm sure if the bank had thought it all out, they would have left the sisters alone. Now, they're stuck with a plot of land they can't sell, and the sisters are virtually homeless.''

''When did they lose the house?''

''About five years ago. So you can see why we're all concerned. They might be tough and a bit rough, but they are really wonderful, and nobody wants to see them distressed, or in pain.

''Anyway, Grandfather and Emma came home upset, spent the next couple of hours trying to come up with a way to help the sisters, and then about two o'clock, Emma looked at the clock, and realized she'd missed her appointment at the beauty salon. Chaos prevailed after that, but she was still determined to go to the dance, even if she had to wear a hat. It didn't come to that, of course. I helped her put rollers in her hair, and as you can see, she looks lovely.''

''What about you?'' Ken asked. ''Have you been looking forward to the dance, too? Or are you here as a special favor to me?''

Jennifer felt her cheeks flush with warmth. "I don't know what you mean...."

"Sure you do. I've seen the faraway look in your eyes all evening."

"Ken, I don't think ..."

Ken reached over and patted her hand. "Don't worry, Jennifer. The subject is dead, as far as I'm concerned. And the last thing I want to do is spoil our evening. Shall we dance?"

Angry at Ken for being so perceptive, and at herself for allowing even one thought of Paul Bishop into their evening, Jennifer followed Ken out onto the dance floor, and went into his arms, where she felt comfortable and secure. And safe.

A few minutes later, when the only thing on Jennifer's mind was listening to the music and following Ken's lead, a deep voice behind them said, "May I cut in?"

Before Ken could respond, or Jennifer could protest, she was in Paul Bishop's arms, staring up into his sapphire-blue eyes. Eyes that were filled with regret.

"I'm going to say this fast," he said, moving Jennifer through the crowd to a secluded corner, "before your date cuts in and tells me to get lost. Or worse, punches me in the nose. I can't tell you how sorry I am that I couldn't meet you for lunch yesterday, but something came up. . . ."

Aware that she should walk away from this man who had managed to uncover feelings and emotions deep inside of her that she hadn't known existed, but unable to do anything but sway to the rhythm of the music and her heart-beat, Jennifer choked out, "For a man who is supposed to be passing through town on his way to South Dakota, you certainly seem to be busy all the time."

"I know, and I'd like to explain, but I can't. I don't expect you to believe anything I say, but I have to try to make you understand. This wasn't part of the plan . . . part of my itinerary."

Jennifer lifted her chin. "*This?* What does that mean?"

"It means I wasn't planning on meeting a beautiful woman. Worse, a woman who could knock me off my pins. If things had worked out differently, I'd be your escort tonight, and we'd be dancing under the stars. . . ." He took a deep breath. "Sometimes, things happen for a reason, Jennifer, and . . . Sorry, but this isn't coming out right. I'll be leaving tomorrow, and I just wanted to tell you I'm sorry, and say good-bye."

And with that, he was gone, disappearing through the crowd like an apparition in white.

White ducks and a white polo shirt, that brought out the dark sheen of his skin . . .

"Jennifer?"

It was Ken, and Jennifer took a deep breath. "I don't know, Ken. I haven't a clue as to what that was all about. H-he's leaving tomorrow, and wanted to say good-bye."

Ken frowned. "He paid five bucks to get into the dance, just to say good-bye?"

Jennifer shrugged. "I guess. Have you seen the sheriff? I should tell him Paul is leaving town. . . ."

"Leaving town with several thousand dollars of the town's money," Ken muttered.

"There isn't any proof Paul is the counterfeiter, Ken."

"I know, and I guess it's just wishful thinking. Guess I'm just jealous. I'd cut off my right arm if I thought it would get you to look at me the way you were looking at him. Well, nuts. The sheriff is over at the refreshment table. I'll wait for you at our table."

Trying to compose herself, wondering how the evening could go from wonderful to dreadful in a matter of minutes, Jennifer made her way to the refreshment table.

The sheriff was talking to a young couple Jennifer had never seen before, but after one look at Jennifer, he excused himself, and pulled her aside. "I don't know if I want to hear this, Jennifer. I saw you talking to Paul Bishop a few minutes ago, and now you're upset. If you could see the expression on your face . . ." He sighed, and waited.

"I-I just thought you should know he's leaving town tomorrow," she stammered, wanting to bite off her tongue for sounding so befuddled.

"And?"

Jennifer shrugged. "That's all. I thought you should know, in the event you want to question him before he leaves."

"I've already talked to him, Jennifer, so you can rest easy. He isn't the counterfeiter."

"How can you be so sure?" Jennifer asked incredulously.

"He just isn't, that's all. He's a man who is passing through, on his way to South Dakota to look at some property. Ah, there's Ida waving me down. Sorry. Gotta go."

Jennifer was still shaking her head when she plopped down at the table across from Ken, and muttered, "My conversation with Paul Bishop went around in circles, and so did my conversation with the sheriff. Have I missed something important? Or am I losing my mind?"

"Well, while you're wondering if you're losing your mind, I'll admonish myself for being a jerk. Sorry. I wanted the evening to be special, not filled with dissension, and—''

Jennifer clapped her hands over her ears. ''I don't want to hear that word again tonight, Ken. Everybody has been telling me they're sorry. Paul, the sheriff, and now you. Nobody has anything to be sorry about. I'm the one who feels wretched for ruining our evening.''

''You didn't ruin it,'' Ken grumbled. ''If anybody is responsible for your sudden gloomy mood, it's Paul Bishop. Now, I suppose you want to go home?''

''I think I'd better, Ken. It's almost eleven, so we won't be cutting the evening too short, and I do have a big day ahead of me tomorrow. Just give me a minute to tell my grandfather and Emma I'm going home, and then—''

Ken waved a hand. ''Do what you have to do, Jennifer. I'll go get the car.''

Jennifer watched Ken push his way through the crowd, and felt a lump form in her throat. He was angry, as he had every right to be. But he was wrong. It wasn't Paul's fault. It was her fault for caring too much, and for being a fool.

It was a little after midnight when Wes and Emma walked into the kitchen, and Jennifer knew the minute she saw their faces that she was in for it.

Emma announced, "Now you can tell us all the things you *didn't* tell us at the dance, young lady. When you told us you were coming home because you were tired. We saw your face. Did you have words with Ken? Or was it Paul Bishop? We saw him talking to you. One minute he was there, and then poof, he was gone."

"He's leaving tomorrow, and he wanted to say good-bye. I told the sheriff, in the event he wanted to talk to Paul before he left, and I still can't figure out what happened after that. The sheriff said he'd already talked to Paul, that Paul wasn't the counterfeiter, so I should rest easy, and then he hurried off, like he couldn't wait to get away from me. At least that's the impression I got."

Jennifer had heated up the dregs in the coffeepot, and Emma made a face. "You need a hot cup of tea, Jennifer, and some solid advice. Get her robe and fuzzy slippers, Wes. She looks frozen clean through. It's either nerves, or she's coming down with some late-summer malady. But my guess would be it's nerves."

Jennifer waited until Wes returned with her robe and slippers, and Emma had a pot of tea on the table, before she said, "I hope you didn't cut your evening short because of me."

Wes said, "It's midnight, sweetheart. And that's late enough for two people our age to be

out and about. We had a good time, and now
we have to find out why you didn't. And I'm
not talking about the sheriff's odd behavior, or
what he did or didn't say.''

"I had a good time. . . ."

Emma harrumphed. "Every time I caught a
glimpse of you, you were either staring off in
space, or had your eyes closed. I think every
single body at the dance could've turned into
little green Martians, and you wouldn't have noticed.''

Jennifer sighed. "You don't have to tell me
what I already know, Emma. But I couldn't have
stopped thinking about Paul Bishop tonight even
if everybody *had* turned into little green Martians. He's been my every thought, day and
night, and it's foolish. No, it's crazy!''

"Affairs of the heart are never crazy," Wes
said gently. "And if you'd rather not talk about
it, we'll understand.''

Emma dropped into a chair and sighed. "And
I'm sorry if I sound like a cranky old lady, but
this isn't like you, Jennifer, and I'll admit it has
me concerned. You are always so levelheaded,
and resourceful, and . . . and . . .''

"And predictable? It's okay, Emma. I understand what you're trying to say. Well, I've always thought of myself as being levelheaded,
too, and that's why I've been so confused. It's

a good thing Paul is leaving tomorrow, because if he were going to stay in town . . .''

"You might have to face falling in love?" Wes asked. "It isn't as frightening as it seems, sweetheart. Actually, it can be wonderful."

"And it could change my life."

"If you fall in love with the right man, the only thing it would do is strengthen it," Emma said, looking at Wes with a special light in her eyes. "When it happens, you'll accept it and embrace it, because the love between a man and a woman is one of God's greatest gifts."

"Amen," Wes said. He studied Jennifer intently. "You know, this isn't too far removed from that time not too long ago when you were afraid to date Ken Hering. Remember? You had a comfortable, friendly relationship with Willy, and then Ken walked into your life, and . . .''

"And I was afraid he was going to complicate my life. I know. And he could still complicate my life if I let him. But I'm not in love with him, Grandfather. And this is different. Don't ask me to explain, because I don't understand it myself."

"Maybe you feel cheated," Emma said thoughtfully. "One day, Paul Bishop walks into your life and knocks your socks off, and the next day he walks out. I can understand that, because that was the way I felt about Billy Docket. I felt cheated and angry. But I got over it, and so will you. Probably a lot easier than I did, because you're not in love with love the way I was.''

Wes stood up and stretched. ''And on that note, I suggest we get some sleep. Tomorrow is going to be a big day for all of us. You have the dog show, I have to be on hand to help close up the fair and the white elephant sale, and I still have a lot to do to get things ready for the barbecue. And poor Emma will be peeling potatoes all day for the salads.''

Emma stood up, too. ''Along with a lot of other women in town. Now, if everybody can just remember who is supposed to fix what, we'll be in pretty good shape.'' Her cheeks dimpled. ''We've got Penelope Davis shucking corn. Figure with those big hands of hers, she can do it in twice the time.''

Jennifer managed a smile. ''Well, maybe she can get her fifteen cats to help.''

Emma leaned over and kissed Jennifer's cheek. ''That's it, honey. Smile. Smile, give thanks to God for the good life He has provided, and remember, tomorrow is another day. Don't fill it with regrets, fill it with new beginnings.''

After Emma went to her room, Wes lingered for a few minutes, and finally said, ''Would you like to go to church to say a few prayers?''

"I'd like that, Grandfather, if you'll go with me."

He gave her a hug. "Then let's go talk to God about new beginnings, and that complicated thing called love."

Jennifer nodded, and took his hand.

Chapter Six

"You know, you have to wonder how this town has survived as long as it has, when you take into consideration that nobody ever agrees on anything," Ben said the next afternoon, while they were setting up for the dog show in White River Park. "I spent a good part of yesterday working at the fair, and can only say it was an eye-opener. I know, I've said that before about a lot of things, and probably more times than I'd care to count, but yesterday seemed to be exceptionally disorganized. And when you stir in a few hot tempers, a mayor who was supposed to be running things and kept telling everybody, 'you handle it,' a sheriff who had to be called out to break up a brawl, said he'd stick around to keep the peace, and then kept disappearing with Paul Bishop, and a concession stand that ran out of food before noon because somebody forgot to put in an order at the market the day before, well, what can I say? Okay, I'll answer that. I'm glad it's Sunday, and that *we're* in charge of the dog show. By this time tomorrow, this jumbled-up holiday will be almost over.'' He looked across the grassy area they had roped off for the ring, to where Tina was trying to keep the overeager dog show participants under control, and sighed. ''Even Tina said she'll be glad when it's over. School starts next Tuesday, and she hasn't even had time to buy school clothes.'' He waved a hand. ''I don't know if you've noticed, but there sure aren't many familiar faces in the crowd. Of course, with the way the town is growing, I guess that shouldn't come as a surprise. Just like that day a couple of weeks ago, when we had a nonstop line of patients coming into the clinic, and we didn't know any of them, or their owners. Guess it's a sign of the times. Well, if nothing else, we're going to have a good turnout. Just hope forty armbands will be enough.''

Jennifer listened to Ben, but her thoughts were on what he'd said about Paul Bishop and the sheriff. She placed the last small, cup-shaped trophy on the table, and said, "Are you sure Paul Bishop was at the fair yesterday?"

"He was there, but like I said, he kept disappearing with the sheriff. Why?"

"Just wondered why he would be there two days in a row."

"Well, I'd say he had business with the sheriff. Saw them together not more than an hour ago, too."

"And just where was that?"

"In that little turnout on the other side of White River Bridge. The patrol car and the van were parked side by side, and they were standing near the patrol car, talking. Looked like they were having some kind of a meeting to me, though I suppose the sheriff could have been giving him a ticket for speeding." He looked at his watch. "It's one o'clock. We'd better get started."

Baffled over the latest development, but with no time to sort it out, Jennifer stepped up to the microphone, tested the PA system, and cleared her throat. "My name is Jennifer Gray. On behalf of my colleague, Ben Copeland, and our assistant, Tina Allen, the young lady in the yellow shorts and blouse, I want to thank you all for your participation in Calico's first dog show, and for providing some sort of verification that your dogs have had all their shots. As I'm sure

you all know by now, this is not an AKC, or
American Kennel Club, event. We don't care if
your dog has a pedigree, or how it performs in
the ring, but we do ask that you keep your dog
on a leash, and under control at all times.

"You've all been given a sheet of paper list-
ing the categories. Look to your right, and you'll
see signs on the grass depicting those categories.
Decide what category you think your dog is best
suited for, and line up accordingly. Tina will
take down the names of your dogs at that time,
and give you a numbered armband that will cor-
respond with the number beside your dog's
name. After that, you can spread around the perimeter of the ring, and watch the judging. When
your number is called, bring your dog to the ring
entrance, and wait. We have ten categories, and
I'll read them off now. The shaggiest dogs, dogs
with tails that curl over their backs, the smallest
dogs, the largest dogs, dogs with the most spots,
dogs with the flattest faces, the fattest dog, dogs
with the shortest legs, dogs with the longest
legs, and last but not least, dogs with the longest
beards. Ben Copeland will judge the first five
categories, and I'll judge the last five. Judging
will begin in fifteen minutes."

Jennifer turned around, and nearly bumped
into Ken Hering, who was standing right behind
her. "I-I didn't see you," she stammered.

"I know. You were too busy dishing out orders. I know you don't want to hear me say this, Jennifer, but I'm sorry about last night. Still friends?"

She smiled, and felt it all the way to her heart. "Still friends. Are you going to take pictures?"

"You betcha. I wouldn't miss this for the world. What if you have a dog that doesn't fit into any of your categories, or if you have a category without an entry?"

"We'll do the best we can, and hope we have at least one dog that can come close. For example, if we don't have any dogs with spots, we'll use patching. No patches, we'll use ticking." She handed him a sheet of paper. "The categories are listed in order, and everybody will get a green ribbon for entering."

"And a stiff reprimand if they don't behave," Ben said. "And I'm not talking about the dogs. I've never seen so much pushing and shoving."

Ken grinned. "Sounds like the rest of the town. Tempers are pretty short. It's been a long week for everybody."

"Too long," Jennifer said. "I have the feeling there will be a lot of changes next year."

A few minutes later, Tina gave Jennifer the list, and tittered. "I sure hope we all survive this. People are coming in by the droves to watch, and if you can believe it, we have a total of thirty-two dogs, and I'd say at least half of them don't fit into any category.''

Ken laughed, and held up his camera. ''Well, if you don't survive, I'll be here to get it down for posterity.''

Tina rolled her eyes, and hurried off to take her place at the entrance to the ring. When she raised her hand to signal she was ready, Jennifer stepped up to the mike and announced, ''Category number one. The shaggiest dog, numbers one through five.''

There was one Old English sheepdog, an otter hound, a cross between the two with a little puli thrown in, and two tiny, fuzzy dogs of unknown origin. The sheepdog was the winner, and Jennifer called the next category. And so it went for the next two hours, until the last category, which was ''the dog with the longest beard,'' and there was only one entry. Jennifer recognized Mayor Attwater's Bouvier des Flandres immediately, and couldn't believe her eyes. His name was Marty, and Ben had delivered him by cesarean section after the pregnant dam had been hit by a car. He was a beautiful, well-cared-for dog, and he was being handled by a pretty little girl with blond hair and big blue eyes, who looked up at Jennifer innocently and said, ''His name is Prince. We're from Omaha. My name is Pam. What's yours?''

When Jennifer and Ben planned the dog show and established the qualification rules, they had made it quite clear that no one who was in charge of any part of the fair could enter a dog. And that certainly included the mayor.

Ben had recognized the dog, too, and joined Jennifer in the ring, muttering, "I hope Attwater has a good explanation."

"Do you have your dog's shot record?" Jennifer asked the little girl.

She pulled it out of a pocket, and handed it to Jennifer with downcast eyes.

Jennifer looked at it, and handed it to Ben. "He cut off the top part that lists the owner's name, the dog's name, and the name of the vet."

Ben walked over to the table, and picked up the mike. "The dog show is over, folks. Congratulations to all the winners, and thanks again for your participation. Now, would the parents of the little girl in the ring please step forward?"

By now, Tina and Ken had joined the group in the center of the ring, and Tina was in tears. "I should've checked closer," she cried. "I should've realized. . . ."

"You were in a rush," Jennifer said calmly, but it wasn't the way she felt. She couldn't believe the mayor would pull an underhanded trick like this! And it was so stupid. Had he really believed they wouldn't recognize the dog? And what did he hope to gain? One small trophy, and one blue ribbon. It was unbelievable.

While Ken busily, gleefully, snapped pictures, Jennifer put those questions to Ben, while they tried to decide how to handle it. And Ben's answers conveyed her feelings exactly. "Just shows you what a jerk he is, Jennifer. Maybe he figured, if you see one Bouvier des Flandres, you've seen them all. Big, gray-brown with a full coat and a terrific beard. The big police dog of France. Like we've got a dozen of them running around town. What a jerk." He took a deep breath. "I know how to settle this one way or the other." He walked a few feet away, turned, and called out, "Hey, Marty!"

The dog bounded away from the girl, and trotted up to Ben.

"Guess that confirms the big debate," Ken said with a wink, as he snapped another picture.

Tears welled up in the little girl's eyes, and Jennifer gave her a hug. "It's okay, Pam. You're not in trouble, but I must talk to your parents. They were asked to come to the ring, but so far . . ."

"They're right there," she said, pointing at the man and woman who were slowly making their way across the ring. The woman was crying, and wringing her hands, and the man's face was flushed with embarrassment.

The man picked up his daughter, and muttered, ''I told my wife we shouldn't do it, but that fifty dollars looked mighty tempting, and with things so expensive, and . . . Well, heck, it was just a dumb dog show.''

Trying to keep her anger under control, Jennifer said, ''Who gave you the fifty dollars, sir?''

The man shrugged. ''Some guy we met in town. Said he wanted to enter his dog in the show, but there were reasons why he couldn't do it himself. He gave us the fifty dollars and the proof of shots, told us to put our little girl in the ring with the dog, and nobody would know the difference.''

Ben said, ''Plump, with pink cheeks, wearing a white or cream-colored suit and a Panama hat?''

''He was plump, and had pink cheeks, but he was wearing dark slacks and a dark shirt.''

The mayor, like Elmer Dodd and his nephew, Collin, had a fondness for light-colored suits and Panama hats, but he obviously hadn't been wearing his infamous uniform that day, and Jennifer could certainly understand why. ''His idea of going incognito,'' she grumbled.

Ben nodded, and gritted his teeth. ''Well, I suggest you take your fifty dollars, sir, and leave. I don't condone what you did, but I can almost understand it. We're living in hard times, and an easy fifty dollars must have seemed like a pretty nice windfall. But I think it's deplorable that you involved your daughter. You must have coached her about what to say, and that's even worse. Don't worry about the dog. I'll see he's returned to his owner.''

After the couple hurriedly left with their daughter, Ken grinned. ''I'd like to be there when 'you return the dog to his owner.' ''

''That can be arranged,'' Ben said. ''And make sure you have plenty of film in your camera. Attwater will be at the Grange at six to officially close the fair, but I have a better idea. On my way over here, I stopped by the white elephant sale to see how the cleanup was going. Wes was there with the mayor, and although I don't have a clue as to what was going on, Wes looked pretty upset. So upset, he called an emergency meeting on the green near the barbecue pit at four, and he all but ordered Attwater to be there. If we hurry and get things cleaned up here, we can attend that meeting, and nail him. I say we make him squirm first, and then go for the jugular.''

Tina was still in tears, and muttered, ''You guys go on. I'll clean up. It's the least I can do after the mess I made of things.''

Jennifer gave Tina a comforting hug. ''It

wasn't your fault, honey. You were in a rush and had to deal with all those people who were pushing and shoving. There is only one person to blame, and that's Mayor Attwater.''

Tina shook her head. ''But why would he do something like that? I mean, it's not like we were handing out thousand-dollar first prizes.''

''Because he's an idiot,'' Ben muttered. ''Always has been and always will be. So what do you think, Jennifer? Do you think Wes would be upset if we crash his meeting? Jennifer?''

Jennifer breathed in deeply. ''I heard what you said, and under the circumstances, I don't think Grandfather would mind at all. Unfortunately, as much as I'd like to go with you and watch the mayor squirm, I have some things I have to do. . . . Um, Emma is tied up at the Mullers all day, making salads for tomorrow, so I have to go home and put the roast in the oven.''

Ben's eyes narrowed. ''And?''

''And then I have to run a few errands.''

Ben grunted. ''Well, from the look on your face, I'd say they must be pretty important errands.''

''They're important. . . .''

''Uh-huh. Then best you get going. We can take care of things here.''

Jennifer hurried out of the park with only one thing on her mind. After getting the roast in the oven, she was going to track down the sheriff and insist he give her a straight answer to the two questions that had been bothering her all day. Just who was Paul Bishop, and what was he really doing in Calico?

A half hour later, Jennifer had the rib roast in the oven, and was on her way out the front door, when the thought occurred to her. The best way to track down the sheriff would be through Nettie Balkin, who was the sheriff's secretary, clerk, and dispatcher, and there was rarely a time during working hours when she didn't know where he was.

Rather than go back to the kitchen, Jennifer went into her grandfather's study to make the call, and had just picked up the receiver when she noticed the unusually heavy scent of honeysuckle wafting through the room, like a window had been left open. It wasn't possible, of course, because Emma always double-checked the windows before she left the house. Jennifer punched in the first two numbers, and stopped. The window screen was on the floor under the window, and the lace curtains were fluttering in the breeze, which meant the window was open!

With her heart pounding up in her ears, Jennifer immediately took inventory. Nothing seemed to be missing, and the wall safe wasn't open, yet she knew somebody had been in the room.

Jennifer quickly went from room to room, but in the end, she was convinced nothing had been taken. The silver was still in a drawer in the dining room, the crystal and china on the shelf, and nothing had been disturbed upstairs, either, or in Emma's bedroom, off the kitchen.

After checking Emma's money jar in the kitchen, and finding it undisturbed, too, she sat down at the kitchen table, and tried to reason it through. Maybe her grandfather had to come home for something, and had forgotten his house keys. No, because he kept the house keys with his car keys, and there was an extra set of house keys in his office at the church. And there was no way he would have taken the time, or the trouble, to climb through a window when he could have walked the short distance to the church. It would have been the same with Emma, too, who also had a key to the church.

With no answer to the dilemma, other than the fact somebody had broken into the house for no apparent reason, Jennifer picked up the phone on the kitchen table, and punched in the sheriff's number.

Nettie answered on the first ring, and her words were clipped and a little breathless.

"Can't tie up the phone, Jennifer. I'm expecting an important call."

With the feeling that if she didn't get it all out in one sentence Nettie was going to hang up on her, Jennifer spouted, "Somebody broke into our house, Nettie, so if you can reach the sheriff or a deputy . . . A report will have to be taken, and the house will have to be dusted for prints, and . . ."

"Why, that's terrible!" Nettie exclaimed. "Well, I'll do what I can, honey, but the sheriff is at the Grange, and under the circumstances . . . Well, I'll try and get a deputy over, but even that might take some time."

With that, Nettie hung up, leaving Jennifer to stare at the phone, and wonder what she'd missed this time. Something was wrong. Very, very wrong, yet for the life of her, she couldn't put it into perspective. She'd known Nettie for years, and had never heard that tone in her voice. Nor could she identify it, which made it even worse. Frightened? Not exactly. Excited? Maybe, but not quite. It was like it was an elusive "something" just out of reach, like a dream you wanted to remember, and couldn't.

Aware that she couldn't touch anything, and she couldn't leave the house with the window wide open, Jennifer resigned herself to the fact she was stuck until somebody came home. She thought about calling Emma at the Mullers, but it wasn't the kind of news she wanted to tell Emma over the phone, so she made a pot of coffee instead, and then slowly checked the house again.

She was going through the kitchen cupboards and drawers for a third time, when Emma walked in, and wearily dropped to a chair. "Lordy, if I don't see another potato for a year, it will be too soon! What are you looking for, Jennifer? I changed some things around in the drawers a few days ago, and you know what always happens after I do that. Nobody can find anything for weeks."

Jennifer quickly explained what had happened, waited until Emma had settled down after venting her rage in her typical "Emma" fashion, which included tossing things around a bit, and calling the culprit every name she could think of that wasn't blasphemous, and then said, "I called Nettie, and she's going to send a deputy to the house, but said it might take some time."

"Have you tried to locate your granddaddy?" Emma asked, pushing her brown, wiry hair off her forehead with the back of her hand, a gesture of pure frustration.

"Grandfather has called some kind of an

emergency meeting on the greenbelt, Emma, so unless I go over there . . ."

"Then go! I'll stay here, and if that . . . that scoundrel, that cur, that despicable lout comes back, I'll be ready for him with a cast-iron frying pan!"

Jennifer tried for a smile. "I don't think you have to worry about the intruder coming back, Emma, but just in case, stay by the phone. I'll tell Grandfather to hurry. Oh, and I'd better leave a written statement for the deputy, in the event he gets here before I do."

"Just go!" Emma exclaimed. "The deputy can get your statement later!"

Jennifer kissed Emma's cheek, and hurried out, with a sick feeling in the pit of her stomach. With the town full of tourists, how could the sheriff possibly find the culprit? And even worse was the thought that it might be one of Calico's residents.

Jennifer reached the parking area behind the church just as Wes pulled in, and it was easy to see he was still upset. Wanting to erase the frown from his face, yet knowing she was only going to add to it, Jennifer gave him a hug as her words tumbled out. "I was just on my way to find you, Grandfather. Somebody broke into the house. . . . Through the window in your study. Nothing was taken, but . . ."

Concern filled his eyes. "Are you okay? And Emma . . ."

"We're fine. We weren't here when it happened. I came home to put the roast in the oven, and found the window open and the screen on the floor. I called Nettie. Apparently the sheriff is tied up at the Grange, so she's going to send a deputy to take the report and do whatever it is that has to be done."

"Boy oh boy," Wes said. "I know that look. What *aren't* you telling me?"

Jennifer sighed. "It has nothing to do with what happened, Grandfather. I just have to talk to the sheriff, that's all. If I thought he would be the one coming to the house, I'd wait here, but that doesn't seem likely. So I'm going to the Grange. I won't be long, and when I get home, I'll tell you all about it. And then you're going to tell me why you had to call an emergency meeting."

His face softened, and his blue eyes twinkled. "Believe me, it wasn't that big of a deal compared to what happened at the dog show. And Ben's little announcement couldn't have come at a better time. By the time he was finished, the mayor was putty in my hands."

On that lighter note, Jennifer headed for the Grange, praying the sheriff was still there, and she could talk to him alone.

Chapter Seven

Jennifer knew there was something terribly wrong the minute she pulled into the general parking area at the Grange. The entrance to the fairgrounds had been cordoned off, for one thing, and the fairgoers, as well as the people who were working at the fair, were being kept behind yellow Mylar tape in a weed-filled clearing to the right of the parking area. And every one of them looked bewildered and frightened.

A tall deputy Jennifer had seen before, but didn't know by name, was there to make sure the crowd stayed behind the tape, and to keep anyone from entering the parking area. He looked all business, and quite capable of using force if he had to, so when he motioned with his hand for Jennifer to leave, she turned the Jeep around, and headed down the road. But she didn't go far. Only to the bend in the road, where she pulled into a little turnout under a stand of trees, and cut the motor. Not in her wildest imagination could she perceive what had happened, but something certainly had, and she knew it was serious.

Jennifer was wondering if she should walk back and try to talk to the deputy, when she heard the approaching vehicle. Moments later, Ken Hering pulled his Bronco in beside the Jeep.

More than happy to see him, Jennifer climbed out of the Jeep, and greeted him with, "I've only been here a few minutes, Ken, but that's long enough to know something is happening at the Grange. They've evacuated the fairgrounds, patrol cars are everywhere, and everything is cordoned off. A deputy is holding a very frightened crowd behind crime scene tape in a field near the parking area, and he's not letting anybody in."

Looking every bit as apprehensive as she felt, Ken returned, "John, Jr., picked up the call through the sheriff's dispatch on his scanner about fifteen minutes ago. It was a 911 call from a neighboring farmer. He said several shots had been fired in the vicinity of the Grange."

"Shots? Oh, no!"

Ken took his camera out of its carrying case, and shook his head. "I know, and I can't imagine. Stay here, Jennifer, and I'll see if I can find out what's going on. I'm the press, and the deputy won't get rid of me so easily."

After Ken drove off, Jennifer tried to reconstruct the scene in her mind. Numerous vehicles in the parking lot. Yellow tape across the entrance to the fairgrounds. Frightened people huddled together, and one deputy to keep things under control. The sheriff's department had eight deputies and six patrol cars, including the one the sheriff drove, and she counted as she recalled where she had seen them. One patrol car near the entrance. Two parked at odd angles to the right of the entrance. One near the field, and two near the entrance to the parking area. All accounted for. So, was the sheriff inside the fairgrounds with the seven remaining deputies? Were they after the person doing the shooting? Or had they fired the shots? If so, who were they firing at?

The parking lot wasn't full. Maybe ten or twelve vehicles, which was understandable. It was after five o'clock, and the fair was scheduled to close at six. The fair, as well as the day, was drawing to an end. Only a few diehards were left, who wanted to see the closing ceremony. The mayor was supposed to be officiating, but she hadn't seen his white Lincoln. But then, maybe he'd parked in the residents' parking area. Was it cordoned off, too? She also remembered seeing a few trucks, a cab-over, and— Jennifer sucked in her breath. A dark green van. Paul's van, and it was parked near the entrance, too, at an odd angle near the patrol cars, like he had abandoned it in a hurry. . . .

With nerves so taut it made her back ache, Jennifer took in deep, cleansing breaths, but even so, she couldn't seem to get enough air. Was it possible Paul Bishop was some kind of a bad guy, and the sheriff and his deputies had him cornered in the fairgrounds? Or maybe he was hiding, and they were looking for him. She thought about all the booths that hadn't been taken down yet, the trailer they were using for an office, and the Grange itself, with its high rafters, lofts, and several small rooms for storage. And what about the arts and crafts people? Were they being held with the others? Or somewhere else? And what about the area behind the Grange, where the arts and crafts vendors had set up camp?

Dizzy now, Jennifer leaned against the Jeep, and closed her eyes. Was Paul the counterfeiter after all? Or was he something far worse, like an escaped convict, or a murderer?

Jennifer had a genuine case of the shakes by the time Ken drove back to the turnout, and his hastily spoken words were far from comforting.

"The deputy wouldn't give me any of the details, Jennifer, but he did say the sheriff and his men are after the counterfeiter. He also said to stay away, or he'd have to stick me behind the tape with the crowd. He meant business, so I wasn't about to argue with him, though I don't intend to leave it at that. This is a story. A big story, and I have the right to be there for the finish."

Jennifer swayed to the beat of her heart. "Did . . . did he say who fired the shots?"

"He said he didn't know, but if you want my opinion, I think he knows exactly what's going down. He was talking to somebody on his portable radio as I was driving away, and it's my guess he was talking to the sheriff."

Jennifer hugged her arms close to her body to ward off the chill, even though the early evening was warm and the air was whisper-soft. "I-I know you probably didn't notice, but Paul Bishop's van was parked near the entrance to the fairgrounds. Sort of cockeyed . . . you know, at an odd angle, like he had to leave it in a hurry."

Ken frowned. "You don't suppose . . ."

Jennifer sighed. "It's crossed my mind, but

there are some other parts of it that simply don't fit, Ken. Ben was working at the fair yesterday, and said Paul and the sheriff were together off and on all afternoon. And then today, he saw them together at that little turnout across White River Bridge, so you tell me how something like that fits in with this?''

They couldn't see the parking area from where they were because of the bend in the road, but the large gray building and the perimeter fencing was visible, and the silos that had been used many years ago to store grain. In between, field grass stretched out like a lion-colored sea against a backdrop of dark-blue sky. It was a beautiful, familiar sight, and Jennifer tried to take comfort in that, and not think about what might be happening inside the fairgrounds.

Ken kicked at a rock. ''I hate this feeling of helplessness, Jennifer, and I hate being kept in the dark. By the way, what brings you out here? Uh-huh, I know. Your important errands. And maybe a little curiosity? I mean, you just said Paul Bishop and the sheriff were together earlier. Wasn't he supposed to leave town today?''

Jennifer managed a wan smile. ''You're a very astute man, Ken Hering. I came out here because I wanted to talk to the sheriff. I knew he was here because I talked to Nettie when I called to report—'' She broke off, and sighed.

"This has really been an exceptionally bad day, Ken. Somebody broke into our house this afternoon. The culprit got in through a window. If he hadn't left the screen on the floor and the window open, I probably wouldn't have noticed it, because nothing was taken that I could see, and when I called the sheriff's office . . . Well, now I know why Nettie said it might be a while before she could get a deputy to the house. And why she sounded so strange. She knew what was happening out here."

Ken shook his head, like he couldn't believe what he was hearing. "Whoa, I guess this has been some kind of day. There was one high point, though, when Ben turned the dog over to the mayor, and gave him what-for. He didn't hold back, either, and Attwater did a lot more than squirm. The jerk tried to stop me from taking pictures, too, and for a few minutes there, I thought things were gonna get physical."

"And I suppose we'll be able to read all about it in the morning paper?"

"You betcha, along with enjoying a very good assortment of pictures. News is news, Jennifer, and the citizens have a right to know what kind of man they've been putting their faith in for so many years. It can't hurt Willy's campaign, either. The mayor and Elmer Dodd are friends, and you know what they say—birds of a feather." He looked off toward the Grange. "I can't do this, Jennifer. I can't stand here with my hands in my pockets, while heaven only knows what's happening. I have to get close enough to take pictures no matter what the outcome."

"You could join the people behind the tape, and take pictures from there."

"I could, but that's not what I have in mind. There is a tangle of bushes and vines on the far side of the parking area, that might give me adequate cover. I'd have a much clearer shot of the entrance from there, and I can always zoom in for close-ups."

"You'll have to leave the Bronco here and walk in."

"I know, but it isn't far, and if I keep to the tree line, and can find enough boulders for cover, I shouldn't have any trouble."

"And you expect me to stay here?" Jennifer asked incredulously.

"I wouldn't mind the company, Jennifer, but what if . . . What if they bring Paul Bishop out in handcuffs, or worse, on a stretcher, or even worse than that, in a body bag? Are you going to be able to handle it?"

Jennifer squared her shoulders and lifted her chin. "If Paul Bishop is the counterfeiter, I can handle it, Ken. And when I think about all the lies he told me. . . . Well, he didn't lie about his dog, of course. Casey was feeling sick that day Paul brought him to the clinic, and—'' Jennifer gasped. ''Oh, no, Casey! Where is Casey?'' Feeling a little light-headed at the thought of the beautiful golden retriever in the middle of a gunfight, she choked out, ''Well, that settles it. I have to go with you, Ken, because Paul Bishop might not be the only one who comes out in need of medical attention. If Casey is injured . . .''

Ken gave her an encouraging smile. ''Think positive thoughts, Jennifer. It can only help us, too. We'll have the advantage because of the position of the sun. If the deputy looks our way, he'll have the sun in his eyes.''

''And in another couple of hours, it will be dark. . . .'' Jennifer swallowed deeply, grabbed up her tote and medical bag, and followed Ken down the road.

''I take it you never leave home without it,'' Ken said, when they'd stopped to rest behind a large outcropping of rocks.

Jennifer checked for stickers on the ground, and sat down, wishing she were wearing sneakers instead of sandals, and that she'd taken the time to change from shorts into jeans. ''If you're talking about my medical bag, no, I don't. I have two of them, actually, and always keep one in the Jeep. Can you see the parking area?''

Ken peered over a rock, and nodded. ''Still status quo. Looks like the deputy is talking on the radio again.''

''How much farther to the clump of bushes you were talking about?''

''Maybe two hundred yards. In between, we have some rocks, a few trees, and a barren stretch of ground about ten feet in diameter. You ever crawl on your belly like a snake?''

Jennifer looked down at her bare legs and grimaced. ''Not since I was a kid. But don't worry, I can do what has to be done.''

''Then I take it you've never played war games?''

''If you're talking about running and crawling all over the countryside shooting red paint out of a pellet gun at an opposing team, no, I haven't. It seems like a pretty silly thing for grown men to do, if you ask me.''

''Don't knock it until you've tried it, and men aren't the only ones who enjoy the sport. I belonged to a club near St. Louis. We had ten female members, and they were plenty tough to beat. John, Jr., and I have been talking about setting up a game one of these weekends. You know, getting a group together and choosing a good location where we won't bother anybody.

We'll end the weekend with a barbecue, paid for, of course, by the losing team. Can you shoot a gun?''

''If you're asking me to be on your team, I'll have to think about it.''

''Well, can you?''

''I've gone target practicing with my grandfather, and I've managed to hit a few cans.''

''Uh-huh, well, I'll remember that. Ready?''

Jennifer nodded, and had just gotten to her feet, when a succession of gunshots pealed through the air. Within seconds, it sounded like a war zone.

''Now!'' Ken exclaimed. ''Everybody's attention will be on the fairgrounds!''

With no time to think, or to consider the possibility of having to dodge stray bullets, they kept low and moved very fast. Jennifer's heart was pounding in her throat by the time they reached the barren stretch of ground, and the shooting had stopped.

''Get down!'' Ken whispered hoarsely. ''Lie flat, and don't move!''

When the gunfire started again, he waved a hand, and they were off again, bolting, finally, into the dense thicket.

Jennifer dropped to the ground, trying to catch her breath, while Ken searched the area for the best place to take pictures.

Now that they were within the safety of the thicket, and listening to only silence as evening shadows crept ever closer, Jennifer's breathing eased, and her thoughts returned to the extraordinary situation they were in. And the reasons that had brought them here. Anything for a story, that was Ken's reason, but Jennifer cared nothing about that. Her only concern was for the golden retriever named Casey, who had had no choice at all in choosing his master.

A few minutes later, Ken dropped down beside her. "So much for one pair of white slacks," he said, pointing at the rip in the knee. "I found a good place to take pictures, but it's in the middle of a blackberry bramble. There is no way you'll be able to get through, and I'm not going to try it again."

Jennifer wiped the perspiration from her brow with the back of her hand, and said, "Then what do you suggest we do?"

"Use the bramble for cover on the far side. If my calculations are right, that should put us even closer to the entrance. Any idea how long it's been since we heard the last shots?"

"Maybe five minutes, though I seem to have lost all sense of time. I feel like I've lived a lifetime this last half hour."

"Uh-huh. That's the way I feel every time I get myself into a pickle."

''Well, one of these days, you'll have to tell me all about your 'pickles,' '' Jennifer said, noticing the big toe on her left foot was swollen. Her legs were scratched, too, and every fingernail on her left hand was broken. Vanity aside, her anger mounted. Paul Bishop had not only put his dog's life at risk, the lives of people she cared about and loved were in jeopardy. If anything happened to the sheriff— Gunshots again, and this time, they sounded very close.

Ken waved an arm, and pointed. Jennifer followed him over the uneven terrain filled with scratchy underbrush, to where the tangle of brambles spilled out in profusion, but also affording them a clear view of the entrance. Crouching low, they waited and listened.

Ken looked at his watch, and held up two fingers. Then three, and then four, which meant that many minutes had passed since they'd heard the last shots. Minutes that seemed like hours to Jennifer, and probably even longer for the sheriff and his men, who were facing untold danger.

Suddenly, there was a commotion at the entrance to the fairgrounds. As Jennifer watched the scene unfold, only one thought came to mind. It was a silly saying or something or other she'd heard and read many times: What's wrong with this picture? What was wrong with it, indeed? She also remembered a line from a movie she'd seen once: "You'd better be prepared, because nothing is as it seems." Three deputies walked out first, followed by the sheriff and two cowboy-type men in handcuffs. It was Tony Sugarman and his father, Victor, the vendors who tooled leather. Tony was also the young man Tina had danced with under the stars, the dark-haired, handsome young man who wasn't *quite* as handsome as Paul Bishop, according to Tina.

Jennifer realized she was holding her breath, and literally gasped for air as Paul walked out, holding Casey on a leash with one hand, and a very large handgun in the other. The remaining four deputies walked wearily behind him, talking among themselves.

Ken was taking a series of pictures, standing tall now, and moving toward the entrance, and Jennifer followed, muttering, "What's wrong with this picture?"

"Looks like we pegged the wrong guy," Ken replied. He looked over his shoulder. "You okay?"

Jennifer nodded, trying to see through the tears in her eyes.

Paul asked her the same question later, after Victor and Tony Sugarman had been loaded into Paul's van, still in handcuffs, and locked in behind a sturdy metal barrier that Cracker Martin would have seen that day they were snooping around the van, had he looked a little closer.

"I'm okay," Jennifer said, looking up into his sapphire eyes. "But you don't want to know what I was thinking when I saw your van, and heard all the gunfire."

He gave her a lopsided grin, deepening the dimple in his cheek. "Bet you thought I was the bad guy, huh? I'm truly sorry, Jennifer. I tried to tell you how sorry I was that night of the dance, but there was no way I could make you understand without telling you the truth, and secrecy was everything. I've been tracking those two for months now, just waiting for them to make a mistake, and I was well prepared to move on to the next town where the arts and crafts show was scheduled to set up next, never dreaming that this was where it would end. Well, I can thank Sheriff Cody for the breakthrough. He went to the fair yesterday in civvies because he was scheduled to work at the concession stand for a couple of hours. He arrived early, and decided to browse through the arts and crafts show, and that's where he was when he saw Victor Sugarman give a wad of bills to a dark-haired lady. He didn't think anything about it until later, when the same lady gave him a bogus ten-dollar bill at the concession stand to pay for a hot dog and a soda. That was when

he put it together. He went to the office and
called the boys in Lincoln, told them what he
had, and demanded they send an agent to Calico. That was when he was told they already had
an agent on the job, and to contact me. He knew
I was on the fairgrounds, and that was a fortunate break, because we had to act fast. We
caught up with the lady in the parking lot as she
was about to leave, and after a couple of hours
of interrogation in the sheriff's office, she con-
fessed to everything. Her job was to pick up a
certain amount of funny money near the close
of each show, and move on to the next scheduled town, so by the time the show arrived, the
town would already be swimming in bogus bills.
If the counterfeit money hadn't been detected by
then, they would continue to pass it as long as
they could. Her mistake was passing that one
ten-dollar bill at the concession stand. She knew
she wasn't supposed to, but she was running low
on the good stuff, and decided to take the
chance. She also told us she was supposed to
pick up another roll of bills today at four-thirty,
and that gave us exactly what we needed to
catch them red-handed.

"The only thing we weren't prepared for was
the gunfight. Victor Sugarman has a rap sheet
twelve feet long, but none of the crimes involved violence, and he supposedly abhors

guns. Well, we can thank the kid for turning that around. Somewhere along the line, he got his hands on a semiautomatic handgun, unbeknownst to his father, and I think he would've done some major damage if he'd learned how to shoot it. A lot of what you heard were wild shots fired in desperation, though sometimes that can be worse than a well-trained gunman with an eagle eye.''

The sheriff stepped up and cleared his throat. ''Don't want to interrupt anything, Agent Bishop, but I was thinking maybe you should call your field office in Lincoln, and give them a report?''

Paul smiled. ''I'd like to talk to Jennifer for a few minutes, so why don't *you* make the call, Sheriff Cody? You can use the cellular phone in the van. Tell them I'll be on my way as soon as I pick up the lady from your jail. And tell them not to worry. The cargo is secure.''

When the sheriff climbed into the van, Jennifer shook her head. ''So that's why the two of you kept disappearing yesterday.''

''Who told you that?''

The sun was down now, but Jennifer could still see the twinkle in his eyes. ''Ben Copeland. He also saw you talking to the sheriff near the White River Bridge earlier today. That was the part I couldn't figure out.''

"With good reason, I would imagine, especially if you thought I was the bad guy."

"That day at the white elephant sale, when you exchanged the twenty-dollar bill for two twenties . . ."

"The girl paid for the teapot with a phony ten, Jennifer. I had to get it from your friend, and then I had to call my office. It was the first bogus bill I'd seen since arriving in Calico, and we had to make plans."

"And do you really live in upstate New York?"

"I do, and I'm not married. Not much chance of a wife putting up with the kind of work I do. But I did lie a bit about Casey. Bad breath, yes, but he wasn't sick. I saw you the day before when they were setting up the white elephant sale, and did some checking. Found out you were a vet, and figured Casey would be the best way to meet you."

Exhausted, and still a bit shaky, Jennifer leaned up against the van, and said, "Which brings something else to mind I don't understand, Paul. You're an undercover agent with the Treasury department, so wouldn't you think you'd be a little more cautious? I mean, you're tall, and impressive, and have a head of golden-colored hair. You own a gorgeous golden retriever, and that strikes me as a most memorable combination, and hardly the image for an all-American undercover agent. Those two guys in the van aren't blind. If you've been following them from town to town . . .''

To Jennifer's amazement, Paul reached up and pulled off a wig. Underneath, his hair was a curly dark brown. And there was no denying, he was every bit as handsome as a brunet.

''I've been using a different wig for different towns and cities,'' he drawled. ''It was the only way. Blond, dark with a gray streak, black, auburn, and even a gray balding job that I hate with a passion. Same with the clothes. A cowboy today, a suit tomorrow, and maybe a biker the day after that.''

''Unbelievable,'' Jennifer murmured. ''But what about Casey? Don't tell me he's wearing a wig, too! Well, no, of course he's not. I examined him!''

Paul chuckled. ''Casey is a part of the team, Jennifer. Along with Hobo, the German shepherd; Othello, the mastiff; Derringer, the black Lab; and Broomhilda, a female Rottweiler. They are all police dogs, and are as interchangeable as the wigs and clothing. If you think I'm blowing my cover by telling you all this, don't worry. Tomorrow, it will be a completely different case, with a whole new set of plans.''

''But you still have to take precautions, which

is why you wouldn't let Ken Hering take any close-up shots of you, and insisted everyone leave the grounds immediately, with the exception of the sheriff.''

"And you," Paul said gently, "because I wanted you to know the truth. But don't worry about Ken Hering. He got a good scoop, and plenty of pictures. He's an okay kind of guy, Jennifer, even if he is a reporter.''

The sheriff was out of the van now, and walked a few feet away, so they could have their last few moments together in privacy.

"And now?" Jennifer asked, barely above a whisper.

"I take my cargo back to Lincoln, and tomorrow is another day." He reached out and touched her cheek. "Be happy, Jennifer. Life is too short not to be. And who knows, maybe our paths will cross again.''

Casey was sitting at Jennifer's feet, and she gave him a giant hug. "If Casey ever decides to give up police work, let me know. He would always have a home with me.''

"I'll remember that," Paul said, climbing into the van. "I'll also remember a night under the stars, that might have been oh so different in a different time.''

Jennifer stood beside the sheriff as Paul drove away, and choked back a thousand tears.

After a few minutes, the sheriff sighed. "Well, this will surely be a day to remember. You okay?"

"I will be as soon as I can find Ken, and tell him he's an okay kind of guy, even if he is a reporter. I have the feeling he isn't very far away. Maybe as far as the bend in the road."

The sheriff grinned. "Would that be the reporter waiting? Or maybe a guy who really cares?"

"Maybe a little bit of both. He probably wants to go home with me, and I can understand that. He probably figures if he sticks with me, he'll have a story a day." When the sheriff raised a brow, Jennifer sighed. "Somebody broke into our house this afternoon, sheriff. I called Nettie to report it, but she wasn't much help. Now I know why."

"Good heavens, Jennifer, why didn't you say something sooner? I could've sent one of the deputies to your house."

"Because this was more important, and nothing was taken. Besides, I'm sure Grandfather and Emma would rather have you take care of it, if you don't mind."

He scowled down at her. "Of course I don't mind, but I'd better get to the house first, so I can prepare them for what they're gonna see when you walk through the door. And then, after all is said and done, you can tell me why you look like you've been crawling around on your belly through briers and weeds.''

Jennifer smiled. ''I'll tell you if you'll give me a lift to my Jeep. It's parked down at the bend in the road.''

Chapter Eight

"Well, it's about time!" Emma exclaimed, when Jennifer and Ken walked into the kitchen later that evening. "The sheriff told us what to expect, but he didn't tell us about Ken." She harrumphed. "Well, wherever you were, you were obviously there together!"

"We were literally crawling through weeds and underbrush on our bellies, trying to get closer to the entrance to the fairgrounds without being seen," Jennifer said, giving hugs around. "And we looked a lot worse than this before we stopped by the Cromwell sisters' to wash up and comb the stickers out of our hair. We had several places we could have stopped in that general vicinity, but we decided on the sisters

143

because we knew they wouldn't bombard us with questions about our appearance. Actually, I wanted to come straight home, but Ken was afraid if I didn't get the scrapes on my legs taken care of, they'd get infected.'' She winked at Ken. ''Of course, that wasn't the only reason. I told him they would probably offer us a glass of their 'elixir,' guaranteed to ease aches and pains, stop hiccups, cure the common cold, and soothe a stressful day.''

Ken winked at Jennifer. ''And Jennifer can't fool me. She wanted to see Peaches.''

Emma looked at Jennifer's legs, and frowned. ''And I suppose the sisters just happened to have a cupboard full of remedies?''

Jennifer grinned. ''And then some. I would have called to tell you we'd be late, but their phone was out of order.''

Wes was frowning, too. ''Crawling through weeds and underbrush while bullets were whizzing overhead. Jim told us what happened, and it's an unbelievable story. Thank goodness everybody is safe and sound, and it's over. I know you probably have a lot more you want to tell us, sweetheart, but it can wait. What you two need right now is a good nourishing meal, and time to unwind. We've eaten, but we have plenty of food left.''

The whole house smelled like rib roast, and

Jennifer's stomach cramped. "To tell you the truth, I'm not very hungry."

Emma scowled. "Jennifer . . ."

"But I'll try to eat something. Where is the sheriff?"

"In the study, going over everything one last time," Wes said. "He dusted the windowsill for prints, but somebody wiped it clean. It's a puzzle, that's for sure, because nothing seems to be missing, and we've gone through the house several times."

"Coffee? Tea? Iced tea or lemonade?" Emma asked.

"Coffee," Jennifer said, "and the stronger the better."

Ken nodded. "Same here."

"I could use a refill, too," the sheriff said, ambling into the kitchen. He'd taken off his tie, and his gray, thinning hair was standing on end, like he'd run his hands through it at least a dozen times. "I can go over everything again, or a hundred more times, but it won't change anything. Nothing was taken and I can't find fingerprint one. Not on the screen, not on the windowsill, or the window. Not even Emma's, which means the culprit wiped everything clean." He sat down and opened his notebook. "Start from when you walked into the house, Jennifer, and give me every detail."

"I walked in, closed the door, and went up-stairs. Approximately five minutes later, I came down to the kitchen to put the roast in the oven."

"That particular window in the study over-looks the front porch. Did you notice the open window when you were on the porch?"

"No, I didn't, but then I was in a hurry. I planned to put the roast in the oven, and then look for you. I was going out the front door when I realized the best way to track you down was through Nettie. I was closer to the study, so I went in there to use the phone. And that's when I saw the screen on the floor, and the open window. I immediately checked the house, but nothing seemed to be missing or disturbed."

"And that's when you called Nettie?"

"Yes."

"From the kitchen?"

"Yes. Nettie said she couldn't tie up the phone because she was expecting an important call, and she sounded really strange. Now I know why. By the way, I don't think she meant to tell me you were at the Grange. It just sort of slipped out."

"Well, if you're worried about me getting on her case, don't be. She's been a gem through this whole thing, and she's kept a faithful vigil by the radio and phone."

Ken looked at the sheriff thoughtfully. "Is it possible Jennifer interrupted the intruder when she came home? She says she went upstairs first. Maybe the intruder was still in the study, and made his escape while she was upstairs."

Emma pursed her lips. "That's a frightening thought."

It was a *terrifying* thought, and Jennifer shivered.

Wes said, "If Jennifer interrupted him, that might explain why nothing is missing."

The sheriff nodded. "And you're sure the window was locked when you left the house this morning, Emma?"

"To tell you the truth, now that I think about it, I don't know. Wes was in a hurry to drop me off at the Mullers, and I was running late. It's possible I overlooked that window."

"And did Wes take you to the Mullers?"

"He did, and Zeke Muller brought me home. Jennifer was here, and you know the rest."

Wes sighed. "There used to be a time when a body didn't have to worry about locking doors and windows."

The sheriff turned the page in his notebook. "I'd say that was a lifetime ago, Wes. Okay, so if Jennifer interrupted the culprit before he could take anything, does anybody have an idea of what he might have been after? Forget that.

That's a dumb question. He could've been after anything from the TV to the silver. Or jewelry, or cash, or other valuables, like art and collectibles.''

''Wes said, ''Which reminds me. Was any of the money recovered from the counterfeiters?''

''Every dime. It's in the counterfeiters' RV. We had the RV towed to our impound lot, where it will stay until the agents from Lincoln arrive on Tuesday to take care of it. At that time, we'll have an accounting of the money, and it will be distributed accordingly.''

''What about the arts and crafts people?'' Emma asked. ''I can well imagine how this must have upset them.''

''They were pretty upset, okay. Victor and Tony Sugarman have been traveling the circuit for almost a year. They were planning to head for South Dakota in the morning, but decided to pull out tonight.''

''So, what are we going to do about officially closing the fair?'' Wes asked.

''Skip it,'' the sheriff said. ''The cleanup committee will be there bright and early, so let's let them have at it, and say we did and don't. Tomorrow is a big day, and I can't see adding to it by dragging everybody back to the Grange. And even if things hadn't turned out the way they did tonight, we wouldn't have been able to have the closing ceremony anyway, because the mayor never did show up."

Wes grinned. "Can't imagine why. You want to tell him what happened at the dog show, sweetheart?"

Jennifer explained, then added, "But I have no idea what happened when Ben confronted him, other than what Ken told me."

Wes said, "There isn't much to tell, actually. Ben made it short and sweet, and all the mayor could do was sputter."

"Wait until he sees the front page in the morning paper," Ken said with a mischievous smile.

"Why did you call the emergency meeting, Grandfather?"

"Because I felt it was necessary to set the mayor straight regarding the barbecue. I still get irked when I think about it. I placed an order with Orris Ford at the meat market for the spare-ribs three weeks ago, and the mayor took it upon himself to cancel it, and order chicken breasts."

Ken said, "And Orris just took the man's word as gospel, and didn't think to clear it with you?"

"If you can believe it, Attwater told Orris he had my approval. Fortunately, I ran into Orris this morning at the fair, and he wanted to know if I wanted the chicken breasts boned. It was also fortunate he had a healthy supply of ribs in the meat locker, so it looks like we're going to have both. I called the meeting because I wanted it understood that the mayor is getting the bill for the chicken, and he's the one who is going to barbecue the chicken, along with supplying the extra barbecue sauce.''

''I don't know, Wes,'' Emma said thoughtfully. ''After all that, and what happened with the dog, the mayor might not show tomorrow. You might have to barbecue the chicken, too.''

''If that happens, we'll all chip in and help,'' Ken said. ''Just don't put me in one of those dumb aprons and screwy hats. Having Elmer and Collin Dodd walking around in their Panama hats will be bad enough, with or without the mayor.''

Jennifer said, ''Speaking of Elmer Dodd, he came by the other night, and offered me mucho bucks if I'd give him back the painting I bought at the white elephant sale.''

The sheriff raised a brow. ''The eagle? Now, why would he do a dumb thing like that?''

Jennifer shrugged. ''I have no idea, but he said I could name my own price. I told him it wasn't for sale. If he hadn't acted like such a twit, I probably would have given it to him.''

The sheriff looked around. ''So, where is the painting?''

"In the storage closet in the hall. I had it in the living room for a while, but I couldn't bring myself to hang it on the wall."

"Is it really that bad?" Ken asked.

"I'll get it, and then you tell me."

A few minutes later, when Jennifer returned with the painting, Ken took one look, and shook his head. "I could do better than that holding the paintbrush with my toes. Maybe it's the frame. Looks like it might be antique."

"Antique, made in China," the sheriff muttered, taking the painting from Jennifer. "No signature on the painting, and no marks on the frame. There has to be more to it, Jennifer. Dodd doesn't part with his money easily, so what would make him offer you a blank check?"

Ken took the painting, turned it over, and placed it on the table. It had a heavy cardboard backing stapled to the back of the frame, and down in the corner, there was a sticker and a price. *Calico Mercantile; $1.59.* Ken frowned. "Well, that's not the price of the frame, and for sure, it isn't the price of the painting. Must be the cardboard."

"I remember that painting hanging above a fireplace in the old Dodd house before Elmer's father passed away," Wes said. "And that was a good long time ago, when the Mercantile was called the General Store. So that tells me the cardboard backing was added after the senior Dodd's passing.''

Emma said, ''So, why would Elmer staple on a cardboard backing, unless . . .''

Jennifer felt her heart flutter. ''Take off the backing, Ken. . . .''

Ken pulled out a pocket knife, began to work at the staples, and finished Emma's sentence. ''Unless there is something of value under the backing, and that's why old Elmer is in such a panic.''

Minutes later, the back was off, and they were all staring at the two folded sheets of yellowed paper. Ken cleared his throat. ''Go ahead, Jennifer. This is your show.''

Jennifer carefully opened the old, dog-eared papers, and frowned. ''They are surveyors' maps of the dairy, but they aren't alike. . . .''

Ken put the painting on the floor so Jennifer could spread the maps on the table, and after a few moments, Wes said, ''I see it, but I don't believe it. Boy oh boy, if this is what I think it is, feathers are gonna fly.''

''If I've got this right, the original dairy lines are here,'' the sheriff said, pointing at the first map. ''But in the second map, they extend to here. Whoa, do you remember when old man Dodd took ten acres away from the Cromwells, claiming the property lines were wrong?''

"I sure do," Wes said. "He hired a couple of top-rate surveyors, and got the proof he needed. That left the Cromwells with five acres instead of fifteen, and there wasn't a blamed thing they could do about it."

"So, what we have here is either the proof he needed, or . . ."

Wes continued, "Or the proof that old man Dodd hired two shady surveyors, and with the help of some corrupt officials in high places, hoodwinked the Cromwells out of their property."

"I don't understand," Jennifer said.

Ken nodded. "That makes two of us."

Emma was studying the maps, and puffed out her cheeks. "My guess is, it's the latter. I remember thinking at the time that there was something fishy going on. The Attwater family owned the property to the west of the dairy in those days, and the Cromwells owned the property to the east. It's my recollection Elmer's daddy went to the Attwaters first, and tried to buy the property because he was in the process of building the dairy, and needed more land. But the Attwaters wouldn't sell."

Wes said, "I remember it, too, Emma. And I remember the old man being fighting mad. Next step was to try the Cromwells, and they wouldn't sell, either."

"You're not talking about the sisters, are you?" Ken asked.

"No," Wes replied. "We're talking about the Cromwell men. Frances and Fanny's father and uncle."

Ken snapped his fingers. "The bootleggers, and you're talking about the old homestead the ladies lost to a foreclosure. Jennifer told me about it, so if what you suspect is true . . ."

"Like I said, feathers are gonna fly."

"But how can we prove it?" Emma asked.

"We might not have to," the sheriff said. "I think Jennifer should tell Elmer what we found, and wait and see what happens."

"But if the records were altered at City Hall . . ."

Wes said, "Elmer's guilty conscience might take care of that."

Jennifer's mind was in a whirl, thinking about the ramifications. "Tomorrow," she said finally. "The place to approach Elmer is tomorrow, at the barbecue. I'll give him back the painting, and then I'll tell him what we found."

Wes nodded. "Well, you won't have to face him alone, sweetheart. We'll all be with you."

Ken was frowning again. "A part of this makes perfect sense, because from everything I've heard, the elder Dodd was a ruthless man. But if Elmer knew about the maps, why did he donate the painting to the white elephant sale? It's almost like he found out about it after the fact, and now he's running scared.''

Wes said, "I'd say that's only one of the many questions we have to ask the man, and with a little bit of luck, we might get the answers.''

The sheriff ran a hand through his hair. "I hate to bring this up, but has the thought occurred to any of you that Elmer Dodd might be responsible for the break-in? If he is running scared, well, desperate men do desperate things. He wanted the painting, Jennifer wouldn't sell it back to him, so maybe he figured stealing it was the only way. I'm not suggesting Elmer did it himself—I think he's too cowardly for that— but what about his nephew, Collin? Or maybe he hired somebody. And maybe it wasn't even a matter of stealing the painting. Maybe the culprit had instructions to remove the backing, get the maps, and then replace the backing. And tell me, who would be the wiser?''

"Who indeed?" Emma said. "Now if somebody will clear the table, your supper is ready.''

Jennifer handed Wes the maps. "I think you should put them in your safe, Grandfather, in case we have a visitor during the night.''

Emma put the salad bowl in the middle of the table with a healthy "thunk." "Let 'em try it,'' she said. "I'll be waiting for 'em with a cast-iron skillet."

Ken grinned. "Want me to spend the night? I can sleep on the sofa with one eye open."

"We appreciate the offer," Wes said, "but that won't be necessary. I'm going to put the painting on the front porch before I go to bed, and if it's gone in the morning, so be it. We'll still have the maps, and that's all that matters."

A plate heaped with sliced roast beef came next, and then bowls of Irish potatoes and summer squash, and a large, crusty loaf of sourdough bread. Jennifer realized she was hungry after all, and dished up generous portions. It was comfort food, and greatly appreciated, because she had the feeling tomorrow was going to be a difficult day at best, and one they weren't likely to forget.

It was near midnight when Jennifer went downstairs to get a glass of milk, and found Wes sitting at the kitchen table. He was still dressed, which meant he hadn't been to bed.

"I take it you can't sleep, either?" Jennifer said, pouring milk into her favorite cartoon glass.

Wes sighed. "I haven't even tried, sweetheart. I've been sitting here for the last hour, trying to find excuses for Elmer Dodd, and wondering what would happen if he actually won the election. The town is growing, and more than ever, we need solid leadership.''

''Do you think he really stands a chance?''

Wes shrugged. ''I don't know. Folks can be funny. Set in their ways, and there are a good many citizens who believe Willy is too young.''

''But if what we suspect about Elmer is true? It could make a difference.''

''Maybe, but would it be fair? Elmer was just a little kid when his father built the dairy, and there is no way he should be held accountable for his father's sins.''

''Yes, but if he knew . . .''

''That's what I've been telling myself. And then, when I put myself in his place, I can almost understand his sense of panic, and yes, of even wanting to cover up the truth, if for no other reason than to protect his father's name.''

''I think you're being very generous, Grandfather. Did you put the painting on the porch?''

''I did, and it's still there. How are your scrapes and cuts?''

''I doctored them again after I took a shower.''

He reached across the table and took her left hand. ''And your fingers? You didn't say anything, but I saw your nails. Broken right down to the quick. I shudder every time I think about what happened at the Grange, and I thank the dear Lord it turned out the way it did. You haven't said, but I gather you and Paul Bishop parted friends?''

Jennifer cast her eyes downward. ''Friends and strangers, Grandfather. I didn't know him. Not as Paul Bishop, the man who was on his way to South Dakota to look at property, and not Paul Bishop, the undercover agent, who was actually on his way to South Dakota in pursuit of the counterfeiters. I'll always remember him as tall and blond, but he was wearing a wig, and Casey wasn't even his. He was a police dog doing a job, just like Paul. A man behind a badge and a gun.''

''Like the sheriff.''

''No, it's different. I can't explain it except to say, I didn't know him, and it's probably a good thing I didn't.''

''But you'll remember him.''

Jennifer felt her throat constrict. ''Yes, I'll remember him. . . .

''We'd better get to bed. Tomorrow is going to be a long day.''

Wes gave her a sly grin. ''Do you suppose I might be able to get to sleep if I drink some milk out of one of your cartoon glasses?''

Jennifer smiled. ''When I brought that set of glasses home from Taco Bell, you had a fit. You said if you wanted to look at Tweety-bird and Sylvester, you'd watch them on TV.''

Wes shrugged. ''When you get to be my age, you get a hankering now and again to change your mind. Just like . . .'' His words trailed off, and he raised a hand. ''You hear that?''

Jennifer heard the bumping noise coming from the vicinity of the porch, and whispered, ''The lights are out in the rest of the house, and the shades are pulled. If it's the intruder, maybe he's trying to find an open window.''

Wes was on his feet. ''Sounds pretty gutsy to me. No time to go upstairs and get my rifle.''

There was no time for anything but to grab up a couple of Emma's cast-iron frying pans, and make their way through the dining room and into the foyer.

When they reached the front door, Wes quickly turned on the foyer light, and opened the door, but they were met with only the sounds of the soft, late-summer night. The intruder was gone, and so was the painting.

Chapter Nine

They couldn't have asked for a better day for a Labor Day picnic and the anticipated barbecue. Feathery clouds played tag with the sun against a bright blue sky, and the breeze, coming off the river, was whisper-soft. The greenbelt along the river had been the place of choice to hold the annual picnic for years, and even though this year the flood had caused the jogging trails to crumble away, most of the area had been untouched. The green itself was a stretch of emerald carpet, bordered by flower-lined pathways, and was used to play organized games. It was also where the badminton and volleyball nets were set up, and where kids could play tag and ball without bothering any of the picnickers.

Individual picnic areas and pathways, tucked in among the many trees, flowers, and foliage, surrounded the green, and the large, community picnic area, containing redwood tables and benches, branched off from the barbecue pit. Beyond that was the parking lot and, finally, the entrance to the nature trails.

It was an ideal setting, and because they'd gotten to the park early, they were able to set up in their favorite spot, which was a shady little knoll overlooking the green, but still close enough to the barbecue pits so Wes would be close by.

And, as usual, they'd brought along canvas lawn chairs, blankets, a picnic basket, and two large ice chests, all filled with an assortment of goodies, even though the town was providing the food.

At the moment, Jennifer and Ken were sitting in lawn chairs, trying to catch their breath after lugging everything up the hill, while Emma met with the salad committee, and Wes officiated the chores in the barbecue pit.

"Not many people," Ken said, looking around.

"It's still early," Jennifer said, pouring two

glasses of lemonade. "Everybody knows the food won't be ready until around noon. Besides, it's supposed to be a lazy kind of day. No hurry, no rush, no fuss."

"Except for the people on the various committees. If I'd known there was this much to putting on what I thought was going to be a simple picnic in the park, I would've volunteered my services months ago."

"Well, if it will make you feel better, there are always plenty of things to do, even if you aren't on a committee. And don't forget, if the mayor doesn't show, you'll be barbecuing the chicken. Meanwhile, relax and enjoy, and take lots of pictures."

Ken's green eyes twinkled. "Did you see the pictures in the paper this morning?"

"I did, and you did yourself proud. You caught the mayor with his mouth in a perfect 'O'. Can't say I cared much for the story, though. I thought it was much too kind."

"Uh-huh, well, that was John, Jr.'s, doing, not mine. He insisted on calling the whole incident a mixup, and insinuating it was only a dog show, and wouldn't it be more constructive to concentrate on the real issues the town must face everyday, than picking on the poor mayor? Of course, that was a lead-in to the next story, which was all about the counterfeiters."

Jennifer sighed. "He must have stayed up all night to get it all in. You got a lot of good photos, Ken, and of the dog show, too. You're a very good photographer."

Ken was wearing shorts, and he pulled an envelope out of his back pocket. "Maybe too good," he said, handing her the envelope. "I zoomed in for a close-up at the Grange last night, and got this."

Jennifer opened the envelope, and felt her heart twist. It was a head shot of Paul Bishop, and the negative.

"I know I wasn't supposed to take any close-ups, but I took it before I got that order, when he was walking out of the fairgrounds, dog on a leash in one hand, and gun in the other. After I left your house last night, I went to my office to develop the film. Had a deadline to meet so we could get the pix in the morning edition. Anyway, when I realized what I had, I knew I couldn't give that particular photo to John, Jr. I was going to destroy it, but then I thought you might like to have it. You haven't mentioned him, and I haven't asked, but I know sadness when I see it. You had the same expression on your face last night that I'm seeing right now. Are you sorry he's gone?"

Jennifer put the photo and negative in her tote. "If you'd asked me that last night, I don't know how I would have responded, but now . . . I'll tell you what I told my grandfather. I didn't know Paul, nor was he the kind of man I would care to know. He was a stranger, passing through town, and he lived in a different world. A lot has happened since last night, Ken. I have a lot on my mind, and believe me, Paul Bishop is far, far down on the list.''

''Uh-huh, well, now that you've brought it up, I knew something important had happened the minute I pulled into the parking lot this morning and saw your faces. Glum. Or maybe even wary. Not the kind of smiling faces I would expect to see on a fine day like today. I didn't want you to think I was nosy by asking a lot of questions, so I decided to wait it out, hoping you'd tell me what was going on, sooner or later.''

Jennifer sighed. ''I said you were an astute man, but maybe 'perceptive' might be a better word. And I was going to tell you right away, but . . . I don't know, Ken. You jumped out of your Bronco with all the eagerness of a guy who was looking forward to spending a fun-filled day, and it's really so incredibly depressing, I can hardly stand it. I just didn't feel like dumping it on your shoulders.''

Ken raised a brow. ''If this is all about confronting Elmer Dodd, I would think that would be the highlight of the day.''

"I thought so, too, until . . . We have a complication, Ken. Remember Grandfather said he was going to put the painting on the front porch last night, before he went to bed? Well, he did. Around midnight, Grandfather and I were in the kitchen talking, and we heard a noise on the porch. . . .''

Ken sucked in his cheeks. ''Whoa. The creep came back and took the painting.''

"That's right. By the time we got to the door, the intruder and the painting were gone. I know, we still have the maps, but this puts a different slant on everything. If Elmer is responsible for stealing the painting, even if he didn't do it himself, by now he knows we know about the maps, and worse, that we have them in our possession, and who knows what he'll do. Will he come to the barbecue and feign innocence when we confront him? Will he stay home because he doesn't want to face us? Or is he at our house right now, tearing everything apart, hoping to find the incriminating evidence?''

"Your grandfather put the maps in his safe, didn't he?''

"Yes, he did.'' She patted her tote. ''He also went over to his office this morning, and made copies. But that isn't the point. Have you ever seen a house after it's been trashed by bur-glars?''

"Unfortunately, I have."

"Well, so have I, and I almost didn't come today because of it, and I know Grandfather and Emma feel the same way. I've already decided I'm going to go home every hour to check on things. Not that much can be done after the fact. Needless to say, I'm on edge, though I'm trying very hard to stay calm."

Ken reached over and squeezed her hand. "Would it help if I told you you look gorgeous? A yellow sundress and sandals, to match the sun."

Jennifer managed a smile. "It helps." Her smile widened. "And that's going to help, too. Take a look at who's coming up the path."

Ken looked over his shoulder, and grinned. It was the Cromwell sisters and Peaches, and the sight of them was enough to put a smile on any-body's face.

The sisters were tall, rawboned women with heads of wiry gray hair and leathery skin, and although they were wearing the usual long black dresses and boots, they'd dressed Peaches in a pink playsuit. Peaches ambled along beside them, holding Fanny's hand, and when she saw Jennifer, her lips pulled back over her teeth in a typical chimpanzee smile.

"Well, now," Frances said. "Fanny said we'd probably find you up here on your favorite little hill. Saw Emma with those other ladies, fussing over the salads, and said hello to Pastor Wes. Mighty fine day for a barbecue, and we're mighty glad to be here, but we wouldn't be if they didn't give us seniors a discount on the food tickets."

"Good mornin' to you both," Fanny said, giving them a brilliant smile.

Peaches had crawled up in Jennifer's lap, and had her long arms around her neck in a death grip. Jennifer held her close, noted she smelled like baby powder, and smiled. "Good morning, to you, too. I take it you're feeling better today, Fanny?"

Fanny nodded, and moved her tongue around in her mouth. "Still have some pain now and again, but it ain't nothing I can't learn to live with."

"I'm glad. Why don't you sit down and re-lax? It's quite a hike up the hill."

"Wasn't much of a hike," Fanny said. "Be-sides, we've got us a bunch of stuff in the back of the truck that needs to be hauled out. We brought along blankets and chairs and prizes for the kids, and extra clothes for Peaches, in case she gets dirty. Oh, and we brought along her pillow and blanket, too, so she can take a nap, and a box of fruit, 'cause we didn't figure we'd find much of that here, exceptin' for the watermelon, and that ain't one of her favorites.''

"Prizes for the kids?" Jennifer queried.

Fanny nodded. "Uh-huh. Last year when we was here, they was givin' out those silly little plastic doodads to the kids for winnin' at the games. Well, we've been workin' on prizes ever since. Good prizes, not that plastic stuff that breaks if you look at it crooked.''

"Like what?" Jennifer asked.

Frances replied, "Like little wooden toothbrush holders that fit right on the wall, and wooden pencil holders, too. And packets of flower seeds so they can start a little garden, and Fanny sewed up some beanbags, and marble bags.''

"Don't forget the knitted bookmarks and all the little packages of brownies, sister," Fanny said. "We was gonna make some cookies, but ran out of flour.''

Frances said, "We were hoping you'd watch little Peaches until we get the truck unloaded.''

Jennifer gave the chimp a squeeze. "I'd love to watch her. Ken can help you unload. . . .''

Frances waved a hand. "Wouldn't hear of it.''

"Well, if you'd like to set up here, we have plenty of room.''

"We thank you kindly for your hospitality," Frances said, "but we found ourselves a little spot on the other side of the green, that overlooks the river. Fanny likes to watch the river meandering by. Reminds her of the time our daddy had a rowboat, and we used to go a-fishing. We won't be gone long. Come along, sister. Jennifer isn't going to take care of Peaches all day."

After they'd gone, Ken shook his head. "Those two are really something."

"I know, and the whole time they were here, I had to bite my tongue to keep from telling them about the maps. I know we can't get their hopes up, but if what we suspect is true, and we can prove it, do you realize what it would mean to them?"

"I can only speculate, Jennifer, and it could go a dozen different ways, but I think one thing would be almost certain. It would change their lives."

Peaches was playing with the buttons on Jennifer's dress while making low gurgling sounds in her throat, and Jennifer laid her cheek against her head. "Their hearts are so big, they deserve the world, Ken."

Ken smiled. "Well, maybe we can give them a tiny corner of it, anyway, and I have the feeling that would be all they'd want." He looked over Jennifer's shoulder, and the smile spread from ear to ear. "I have the feeling we're in for a lot of surprises today, too. The mayor is at the barbecue pit, and he's wearing an apron."

"Good! Maybe he figured if he didn't show, the next thing on the town council's agenda would be to have him tarred and feathered."

Jennifer breathed in deeply of the sweet scent of flowers and the aroma of barbecue wafting through the air, and began to relax, in spite of problems they still had to face. Today would be yesterday, tomorrow, and it would be gone for- ever.

"Get the loaf of day-old bread out of the pic- nic basket, Ken, and let's take Peaches to the pond, and let her feed the ducks."

Ken raised a brow. "You think that's wise?"

"It isn't only wise, it's absolutely necessary. And then after that, we're going to take her wad- ing in the kiddie pool, and after that . . ."

"Whoa," Ken said. "Let's get through the ducks first, and if we survive that, we'll talk about moving on."

Jennifer smiled, and headed down the trail.

By three o'clock that afternoon, the picnic could only be called a complete success. Almost everybody in town had been there for at least a little while, and the barbecue and food had been outstanding—even the mayor's chicken. And who would ever forget the Cromwell sisters when they announced they were taking over officiating the kids' games, as well as some of the adult games, and finally, when they'd handed out all their wonderful prizes to the winners?

Ken had taken some terrific pictures throughout the day, and now, with nothing more to do but spend a few lazy hours before it was time to go home, Jennifer, Wes, Emma, and Ken were sitting on their little knoll, talking about how well the day had gone, but skirting around what was really on their minds. Elmer and Collin Dodd had been conspicuously absent from the festivities, and although they had hardly been missed, it presented a whole new set of problems. And the biggest question of all was, where were they? Home, behind locked doors, planning some sort of a defense for the trouble they were in? But no matter what they were up to, they hadn't attempted to get to the maps, because each time Jennifer had gone home, the little house beside the church had been safe and secure.

Finally, Emma spoke her mind. "A lot of the folks are leaving. Do you think we should stay until the end, in the event Elmer shows up? Or do you think we should call it a day, and see what tomorrow brings?"

Wes said, "I don't think Elmer is going to show, but I'm not ready to go home yet, either. It's been a fine day, much better than expected, and it's nice here. Relaxing. And for the first time in days, I don't have to worry about what has to be done tomorrow."

"Amen," Emma said. "But I can't forget about all the housework that needs to be done. Things I've been putting off because of the fair."

"My office at the church is in a bit of a mess, too," Wes said. "And . . . Boy oh boy. I guess we have one more hurdle to jump before this day is over. Elmer Dodd is coming up the hill, and he's headed our way."

The hill wasn't long, nor was it steep, but by the time Elmer reached the top, he was winded.

Wes pulled out a chair. "Elmer. You'd better sit a spell, and catch your breath."

Elmer sat down and mopped his brow with a handkerchief, and the first thing Jennifer noticed was the expression in his dark eyes. He looked defeated. There was no other way to describe it. And then there was his clothing. Wrinkled slacks and a wrinkled sport shirt; it was apparent he wasn't trying to impress anybody today.

He stuffed the handkerchief into his shirt pocket, and looked at Wes. "I didn't know if you'd still be here, but I took the chance. Ran into Ben Copeland, and he said you were up on the knoll above the barbecue pit. . . . I have to talk to you in private."

"Whatever you have to say can be said in front of everybody here, Elmer."

Elmer scowled. "You're not going to make this easy on me, are you?"

"It depends on what you're talking about," Wes said. "But I think I'd better tell you, we want to talk to you, too."

The scowl deepened. "I don't like the idea of talking in front of a reporter."

"Ken is a good friend, and he isn't here as a reporter."

"Would you like a glass of lemonade, Elmer?" Emma asked. "You look like you could use something cool to drink."

Elmer nodded, and cleared his throat. "We go back a long way, Wes, and I've always known you to be a fair and understanding man. I'd like to think you'll continue to be, no matter what I have to say."

Jennifer held her breath. Was the man going to confess?

Ken spoke up. "Maybe I'd better go. This sounds like a personal conversation, Mr. Dodd, and if you'd be more comfortable . . ."

Elmer studied Ken for a few moments, and shrugged. "I guess it doesn't matter, one way or the other. This is going to come out sooner or later, and the whole town will know. You'd might as well hear my side of it. What you think after that is your business.'' He cleared his throat again. ''I took the painting of the eagle off your porch last night, Wes. I'd spent the evening driving around thinking, and I guess it was about midnight when I drove by the church. Saw some lights on in the house, and decided to stop. All I intended to do was try to talk Jennifer into selling me the painting, or if she wasn't up, ask whoever was to try to talk her into it. But when I got to the porch and saw the painting just sitting there, well, I guess I went a little nuts. I took the painting and went home.''

Wes said, ''Only it wasn't really the painting you were after, was it?''

He shook his head. ''I won't go into what happened when I got home and took the backing off the painting. Now you have the maps, so I guess my only question is, what are you going to do about it?''

''It depends on the answers you give us,'' Wes said.

''So ask.''

''Why don't you just start at the beginning, and tell us the truth?''

''There isn't a beginning,'' Elmer muttered. ''Only the end. I've always hated that picture.

Even when I was a kid, I hated it. But my daddy liked it, and so it stayed up on the wall. After he died, I stuffed it away with all the relics he'd collected over the years, and never gave the blamed thing a second thought, until last Friday, when my brother Roland called from Omaha to find out how I was, and how the big week was going. That's when I told him about the stuff I'd given to the white elephant sale, which included the painting. Well, I can tell you, I've heard Roland angry before, but not like that. He was screeching so loud, I had to hold the phone away from my ear. When he settled down, he told me in no uncertain terms to get the painting back, and why. I went to the sale, but Jennifer had already taken the painting home. Well, you know the rest.''

''Only that you came to the house, and offered to buy back the painting, and Jennifer could name her price,'' Wes said. ''Didn't you think that would make us a little suspicious?''

''I wasn't thinking, Wes, and that's the honest truth. When Roland told me what happened years ago, it about killed me, and that's the truth, too. I didn't believe it at first, but then I had to, because why would he lie about something like that?''

''I assume you're talking about the fraudulent

map giving your father a ten-acre plot of land that didn't belong to him?''

Elmer's shoulders drooped. ''That's what I'm talking about. Roland and I were the only kids, and Roland was the oldest, by some ten years. And he knew all about it when our daddy hired those dishonest surveyors, and paid somebody at City Hall to falsify the records. But it wasn't until our daddy was dying that he asked Roland to get rid of the maps. But he didn't. He said that only a fool would get rid of something important like that, because someday, it might come in useful. That didn't sound like good reasoning to me, but then that's Roland. Always thinking of ways to spear somebody through the heart, and in all probability, it would've been my heart. You know, someday when we have a falling out, and he wants to do me under.

''Anyway, he knew how I felt about that painting, but he also knew I would never get rid of it. After Daddy died, I told him I was going to put it down in the basement with the rest of the relics, where it would stay for all eternity. So I guess he figured that was the safest place to put the maps. Don't ask me why he didn't take them when he moved to Omaha. I asked, but he wouldn't tell me. Probably figured it would be smarter if he left them with me. Then his hands would be clean, so to speak.

"About all I can do is swear to you I didn't know anything about it until that call. But I truly did understand the significance of what Roland was saying. And that's why I had to get the painting back. In the wrong hands, I'd be ruined, and our daddy's name would be ruined. He might have been a lot of things, but I loved him."

Tears filled Elmer's eyes, and he blinked them away. "Now it doesn't matter. Nothing matters."

Wes took a deep breath. "You can't be held accountable for your father's, or your brother's, misdoings, Elmer. But you must be held accountable for yours. Are you aware that somebody broke into our house yesterday?"

Elmer frowned in puzzlement. "Well, I'm sorry, but what does that have to do with anything?"

"Well, not more than a few days before, you were begging to buy back the painting at any price, so it occurred to us that you might have broken in to get the painting, or that you hired somebody to do it. Nothing was taken or disturbed in the house, so it's possible Jennifer interrupted the intruder when she came home unexpectedly. Entry was through an open window in my study, and she went straight upstairs, so if the intruder was in the study at the time, he could have easily gotten away undetected. He was also very careful, and wiped everything clean, including the windowsill.''

Elmer was shaking his head vigorously. ''I swear to you, it wasn't me! I had nothing to do with it!''

''What about Collin? Does he know about the painting and the maps?''

''Well, yes, of course, but he wouldn't do something stupid like that. He might be shiftless and lazy, but he isn't a thief.''

''Not even on your behalf, if he thought he was doing you a favor?''

Elmer sighed. ''Well, even if he did, you think he'll admit to it? No way. I'm supporting him nearly one hundred percent, and he sure wouldn't do anything to jeopardize that.''

''Maybe he wasn't planning on telling you. Maybe the whole idea was to get the painting, and destroy the maps.''

Elmer shook his head. ''This is going around in circles, Wes. You think Collin did it, and I don't. But you still haven't answered my question. What are you going to do with this information?''

''That's not my call to make, Elmer. All I can do is advise you. If you want to correct this dreadful situation, then I suggest you make it up to the Cromwell sisters. The Cromwells were duped out of ten acres.''

Elmer heaved a ragged sigh. ''Are you suggesting I give them ten acres of my dairy?''

''No, I'm not suggesting that at all. I doubt very seriously that they would have use for ten mucky acres of dairy land. A total landfill wouldn't be able to correct those problems. But I am suggesting you pay them for the ten acres, taking into consideration current property values and interest.''

It was easy to see Elmer was calculating dollar signs in his head, and his face grew pale. ''That would cost me a fortune, Wes.''

''A fortune you can well afford, when you consider your options.''

''Meaning?''

''Meaning, unless you do the right thing, there is no way I can sit on this information, and simply forget it. If you do the right thing, it can end here.''

''And if I don't? That's blackmail, Wes!''

Wes scowled. ''I would hardly call it blackmail. Don't turn this around and make me the bad guy. We all want to see justice served, and you have the ability, and the money, to make it happen.''

''Then I don't have a choice.''

''I'd say, that's about it.''

"So what do I tell the town when the crazy Cromwell sisters suddenly end up with megabucks, and I'm destitute in the streets?"

Wes smiled. "I can hardly see you 'destitute in the streets,' but if you're dead set against telling the truth, a simple solution might be to tell everybody that way back when, there was a mixup in property lines, and it has come to your attention that ten acres of your dairy belongs to the Cromwells. I don't think it would have to go beyond that."

Elmer swallowed. "Yeah, well, how much do you want to bet everybody puts that together in a hurry?"

"Since when do you care about what people think?"

"So, what do I do? Walk up to the Cromwell sisters, hand them a check for X number of dollars, and say, 'Sorry, but my daddy took ten acres from your daddy X number of years ago, and now you're rich, and I'm poor?' "

Wes had to smile at the man's insolence. "I think it will be a little more complicated than that. First of all, we'll get a lawyer to handle it, including the necessary paperwork."

"Like Willy Ashton? Wouldn't that be a conflict of interest?"

"No, not Willy, but we have several other good attorneys in town. It wouldn't take long.

Once the papers were drawn up and the correct figures tallied, that would be the time for the signatures, and to write out the check.''

Expecting Elmer to say, ''I'll think about it,'' Jennifer heaved a sigh of relief when he said, ''Don't suppose I can use my lawyer?''

''It wouldn't be advisable,'' Wes replied. ''Let me make some calls in the morning, and we can go from there.''

''And the maps?''

''They stay in my safe until the ink is dry on the papers, and the check.''

Muttering to himself, Elmer stalked off down the hill, and the sighs around were audible.

''Lordy, if that isn't the ticket!'' Emma exclaimed.

Ken reached over and shook Wes's hand. ''You handled it splendidly!''

Wes shook his head. ''It doesn't feel splendid. It feels sad. With all of it, I feel sorry for the man.'' He looked at Ken. ''How are you going to handle this, Ken?''

''You mean because I'm a reporter? I'm also your friend, and I'll handle it anyway you want me to.''

Wes finally smiled, and it reached his eye. ''Well, after we get through the formalities, maybe you can take some pictures of the sisters receiving the check from Elmer. Unfortunately, without the whole truth coming out, it's bound to put a few more votes in his corner. A lot of folks will applaud him for doing the right thing.''

"It doesn't matter," Jennifer said. "Willy can handle his opposition, no matter how many extra votes Elmer gets, and when you think about the outcome . . . Oh, Grandfather! Think about what this will mean to the sisters! They can get their teeth fixed, and get insurance, and maybe even buy the old homestead back from the bank. They can get a decent vehicle, and . . .''

Ken chuckled softly. "And maybe even by a rowboat, so they can go fishing."

When Emma frowned, Jennifer laughed. "When the sisters were here earlier today, Frances said they were setting up on the other side of the green where Fanny could watch the 'meandering' river. And she talked about the old days, when their daddy had a rowboat, and they used to go fishing."

Emma harrumphed. "Put those two in a rowboat now, and they'd probably fall overboard. Hmm. The last I saw of them, they were over near the duck pond. Seems Peaches has taken a liking to feeding the ducks, and she doesn't want to leave. Why don't you go tell them the good news, Jennifer? And then we can all go home.''

Jennifer got up, and put out her hand. ''Come with me, Grandfather?''

Wes took her hand and smiled. ''It would be my pleasure, and the perfect end to the day.''

As they walked down the hill hand in hand, Jennifer lifted her face to the breeze, and felt her heart swell with happiness. No, they couldn't give the sisters the world, but they could give them that tiny corner, and it truly would be enough.